How They Came To Be

THE **4**MIDABLES ADVENTURE SERIES

Book One

DON YOUNG

ILLUSTRATIONS BY
Midjourney

www.the4midables.com

Cover Artwork by VisualPulse

Illustrations by Midjourney

Paperback ISBN: 978-1-0689685-1-8

Ebook ISBN: 978-1-0689685-2-5

Hardcover ISBN: 978-1-0689685-3-2

I'm excited you're about to read my first novel! Before you begin I want you to know why I created these characters and stories. I was fortunate to write for the 'Inspector Gadget' cartoon series, which became an international hit. In his efforts to catch the bad guys, Gadget didn't have a gun, and he never killed anyone. I believe there's too much violence on TV and in films for young viewers, so I created THE 4MIDABLES as a live-action, superhero TV series. But these 4 teens don't have *real* superpowers, just a really cool 'device' they use to help people they don't even know, while never revealing to the world who they are - even their parents!

Many writers submit scripts to *The Black List* in Los Angeles to have industry professionals provide feedback prior to meeting with Producers. Here's two Reviews of the Pilot script for my proposed TV Series.

This is a very engaging superhero adventure, with the clear Good vs. Evil dynamic serving to make this an appealing option for families. The premise is a lot of fun … and the concept could certainly carry on with seasons worth of drama.

The concept is what makes this script stand out -- the teens can travel all over the world and make it home for dinner! It's elevated by some smartly crafted elements. The casting is diverse in terms of its global audience appeal.

You're all set to meet THE 4MIDABLES! They're really good people I know you'd love to be friends with.

Be sure to check out my exciting news on the last page!

<u>In Memory of</u>

Eli Rill * Larry D. Mann
Lew Weitzman

1. MEET THE GILLER'S

A sunny morning greeted the 35,624 residents of Merritt Island, Florida, a community in Brevard County, six miles from the John F. Kennedy Space Center. In his first State of The Union address in 1961, the 35th President of the United States made the shockingly bold statement that the US would send astronauts to the Moon, and bring them safely home, before the end of that decade. Kennedy's challenge was spurred by his desire that the US could not let the then Soviet Union be the first country to plant its flag on the Moon's surface.

Inside the tidy bungalow at 16 Fairfield Road, seventeen year old Madison Giller, fresh from a shower after her two mile jog, waits for the blender to finish its work on the fresh melon, bananas, apples and oranges she's just cut up. She was twelve when she abruptly stopped eating meat and consuming sodas, embarking on a meticulous diet that favors fish, pasta, eggs, fruits and veggies. It keeps her lean, trim frame in top shape as captain of her high school *Rebels* soccer team.

Her prowess on the pitch, plus her 3.6 GPA, has attracted heavy scouting from the nation's top soccer programs, but she carries herself with a humble, kind vibe her friends admire. She's rarely in a dress and heels as she prefers casual attire, comfy shoes and funky caps. And the color in her cheeks is Sun-sourced, because she never wears makeup. She relishes her role as the one who keeps her brother and father well-fed, and their middle-class home neat and tidy. The family really misses Mom, a professor at Stanford University in Palo Alto, California, who gets home once a month for weekend visits. The blender's loud work now completed, she turns to the hall and shouts, "E!"

Her brother, Ethan, has been in the basement for over an hour reading his Dad's science journals in his office-laboratory with work benches, computers, bunsen burners and rabbits in cages. He's sixteen months younger than his sister and his passion is science, as his Dad has encouraged him to dream the unimaginable. He doesn't have time for sports and hangin' at the Mall because he's on a mission to be a great scientist like his dad. He's barely a hundred and forty pounds and hates exercising almost as much as combing his blond hair which he prefers covered by hoodies or ball caps. He gets up and looks at the hamster wheel with a determined resident. "Have a great day, Harry." he grins at the grey hamster, walking past a framed photo of astronaut Neil Armstrong on the wall, and several NASA awards around it. He bounds up the stairs and walks into the kitchen.

"Hey, Mad." as she hands him a glass of fruit smoothie."Thanks." grabbing two slices of whole wheat and the PB jar.

"Morning, guys." greets dad, one of the world's most renowned molecular physicists, and affectionately known by everyone as Dr. G. His fascination with science began at age 3 flipping through his Dad's science books. By age 8 when his school chums were trading baseball cards, his 'stars' were Sir Isaac Newton and Albert Einstein. His 162 I.Q. got him into Massachusetts Institute of Technology a month after turning *twelve*. Graduating from the famed institute at seventeen with his Masters in Molecular Science, he was hired by NASA to study the effects of orbital travel on astronauts. He's a soft-spoken man with a kind demeanor who enjoys a close bond with his children, encouraging Madison in her athletic pursuits and nurturing Ethan's scientific interests. He sits beside Ethan, making his fave PB and banana slices sandwich."What's your day, Ethan?"

"Gonna start studying for my Physics exam."

"When is it?"

"This afternoon." taking his first bite.

"You're so lucky, E." says his sister, sitting down, sipping her smoothie. " I could study a hundred hours and never understand those numbers."

"You're doing alright. You got mom's beauty and athletic ability." says Dad. Madison smiles her thanks. "What's your day, Dad?"

"Working on the Mars Mission." he smiles.

* * *

Walker High Secondary is a six-minute bike ride from home for Madison and Ethan. Most days they're joined by Madison's closest friends, and *Rebels* teammates, Rebecca and Natalie. Rebecca and Madison have been best friends since her family moved down the street from the G's nine years ago. She loves reading romance novels, watching Tik-Tok and Insta videos and playing soccer. She's not as extroverted as Madison, and thinks of her like a sister. Natalie thinks it'd be very cool to be a movie star. Her hobbies are buying clothes, watching movies and sleeping in on weekends. Today, Garret is riding with them. He's a science geek and Ethan's only close friend. They spend hours together working on science projects in Ethan's lab in the basement.

"My Tik-Tok post of Rufus standing on his hind legs barking got 117 likes and 47 shares." says Rebecca.

"He's so adorable!" smiles Natalie. "Do you know Tik-Tok had 22 *trillion* minutes of views last year and Netflix had I think it was only seven Trillion."

"Really? says Madison, as they hop off their bikes at the bike rack.

"Taylor cracked 250 mil' on insta?" says Rebecca.

"I'd be so lit if I had a thousand! says Natalie, as they walk on.

*　*　*

That afternoon Madison and her two BFF's are on the pitch doing a cool-down jog following a *Rebels* soccer practice. Madison is a left winger and central attacking midfielder. Her sixteen goals in twelve Matches this season is tops in the Conference and the *Rebels* sit atop the standings with a sterling 10-0-2 record. For two seasons she's been on the radar of all the Top NCAA soccer powerhouse programs, including Florida State, UCLA, UNC's Tar Heels, Duke and Stanford. But Madison's heart is set on playing for Stanford and pursuing a career in environmental studies like her Professor Mom. It would also allow her to live with Mom in Palo Alto.

"Cardinals are ranked number one." says Madison."Two sophomores are starting, so they'll be seniors when I get there. Tough roster to crack."

"You could turn some heads." says Rebecca.

"But if I don't I'm red-shirted. Anyway, I have to put my Degree first. It's gonna be my life's work." Natalie holds an imaginary microphone, mimicking a TV reporter. "There you have it folks, soccer star Madison Giller's next big goal is saving the world from the ravages of our depleted environment."

"Yeah, right" grins Madison, as they jog off the pitch.

* * *

Dr. G is standing at the barbecue on the backyard deck, as Madison bikes up.

"Hey, Dad!" as she hops off.

"Hey, Mad'. How was your exam?"

"It was okay. Thought we were doing pizza tonight?"

"We have a special guest …"

"Hi, dear!" smiles mom, walking onto the deck. Madison is shocked. "Oh, my gosh!" running to give her a big hug.

Mrs. G is a smart and fiercely independent woman who has had a fascination with the environment since a trip to the Brazilian Rain Forest as a teenager. She loves her family very much, but Stanford's offer two years ago of an Associate Professor was too good to turn down. So their visits to Palo Alto, and her visits home, are special occasions. She has little interest in material things and is as happy sleeping in a tent beside a lake under the stars as she is in her comfy bed at home. Her children are the most important part of her life and she's delighted Madison has her passion for the environment, and Ethan has his father's passion for science.

"You came a week early?" walking arm-in-arm with mom to the barbecue where there's three large burgers on the grill and something wrapped in foil.

"Dad's ready to reveal what he's been working on and couldn't wait a week to tell you."

Madison looks at her dad like a kid on Christmas morning. "This is so exciting, Dad!"

"You have no idea how excited I am." he grins, as Ethan walks up. "Dad's telling us what his secret experiment is!" Madison gushes.

"Seriously?!" looking wide-eyed at his dad. "I'm too excited to eat now."

"No, the burgers are ready, and I cooked salmon and asparagus for Mad'."
Ethan looks at his sister. "Eat fast!"

Not even thirty minutes later, Dr. G has assembled the family in his basement laboratory. Madison and Ethan can barely contain their excitement.

"What I'm about to show you must remain our family secret. You can't tell anyone."
Madison and Ethan nod, busting to hear.

"Mom's work is very important to her, but we miss her terribly, and it's very long flights home every four weeks. So I've created a way for us to teleport anywhere in the world, in seconds!"
Madison and Ethan are astonished!

"Teleporting?!" says Madison.

"Seriously?! How's that even possible, Dad?" says Ethan.

"I had to find a way to temporarily reduce our body mass prior to porting."

"I'm having some very gross thoughts." grimaces Ethan.

"Ewww, E!" says Madison.

"It's not that extreme. I created a pill you swallow, without water." He shows them a pill. "It creates a reverse metamorphosis in your body within thirty minutes, and then you're ready to teleport."

"What's in the pill? Ethan asks.

"For security reasons I prefer you not know. But they're expensive to produce. Fortunately the effects last twenty-four hours."
Madison looks wide-eyed at her smiling mom.

"For the digital software I was going to program a cell phone, but they can easily be lost, and you know how I'm prone to losing things." he shrugs.

"Digital software?" asks Ethan.

"To input your destination." Dad opens a cabinet and takes out what looks like a soft cast for a broken arm. He slides it easily over his left forearm. "I went with the sleeve for secrecy, and it's harder to lose. Just inside the sleeve is a small button you push." He puts his index finger inside the front of the cast near his wrist and a small panel slides open revealing an iPhone-size keypad.

"The keypad is very similar to your iPhone and has numbers 1 to 10, and star and number signs to enter your GC's."

"GC's?" asks Madison, her brow furrowed.

"Global Coordinates for where you want to go."
Madison and Ethan have a million questions!

"Where do we get them?" asks Ethan.

"Online. Every physical location has its own digital address from satellites. Be very careful entering your GC's. I was so nervous on my first test flight to visit mum I inadvertently entered an incorrect number. I was 37 miles off and landed in San Francisco." looking sheepishly at Mrs. G., who grins.

"Oh, my gosh!" chuckles Madison.

"Fortunately I didn't land in the Bay! I'll tell you why in a minute."

"So how do you land?" asks Ethan.

"I'm getting there. Okay, now before you launch, you take a very deep breath and forcefully exhale every last ounce that you can." He inhales deeply and then very forcefully strains to release as much as possible. "Then you quickly press the pound key. The panel will close and 2 seconds later you vanish into thin air!" He snaps his thumb and finger. "Arriving seconds later at your destination," he grins and unfolds his arms wide, "with zero side effects." Ethan and Madison are wide-eyed!

"Oh. My. Gosh!" exclaims Madison.

"How many times have you teleported?" asks Ethan.

"Yesterday was my 34th flight. I had lunch with mom at Mount Rushmore!" Mom shows them a selfie they took with the 60-foot tall heads of four of the greatest US Presidents looming behind them; George Washington. Abraham Lincoln. Thomas Jefferson. Theodore Roosevelt.

"And you were home for dinner!" says Ethan.

"That's why you weren't hungry!" grins Madison,

as her dad nods.

"So we can we go *anywhere* in the world?" asks Ethan.

"Yup. We've been to Africa, Spain, England …" looking at Mrs. G.

"New York, Rome, Hawaii." adds mom.

"I wanna go to Paris and Brazil!" grins Madison excitedly.

"Africa for sure!" says Ethan.

"Wherever you want."says mom, looking at her kids, giddy with excitement.

"This is so amazing!" Madison grins.

"Now, you must be outside to launch because you can't teleport through a solid mass. And you can't launch in the rain." says dad.

"Or if you're floating in San Francisco Bay." grins mom.

"What if we're ready to come home and it's raining?" asks Madison.

"Take a train, bus, or taxi to some place nearby where it isn't raining."

"What if there's a mechanical malfunction?" she asks.

"You can't call the Auto Club." grins Ethan.

"Before you port you'll download your GC's to my server so I know where you are. I'll Port there with a back-up cast-sleeve. I've made several."
He grab two Sleeves from a cabinet. Madison and Ethan are very excited sliding on their Sleeves.

"Now, we'll be porting 1,000's of miles from

home and we need to be able to communicate." dad continues. "We can't use our phones because it would trigger big roaming charges for calls and texts we make and receive."

"But the bigger problem," adds mom, "is if we're in three or four countries in one day it would trigger a fraudulent activity alert by Verizon."

"Yeah, how could we be in four countries in a day?" says Madison.

"Guess that means no credit cards too, huh?" says Ethan.

"Exactly. So to replace our phones …" he takes out a tiny, flesh-colored computer chip. "This is a digital audio chip our Mars astronauts will use - DAC for short. You place it in your ear canal." He places the DAC in his right ear and secures it. "It has an adhesive that keeps it securely in place. I've linked the chip to the GPS in your sleeve."

"How do we dial?" Ethan asks.

"There's no dialling." dad grins. "You speak and Madison hears you wherever you are!"

"Oh, man! We've got the coolest phone in the world, Mad'!" Ethan says.

"I can't wait to try it!" grins Madison.

"It's very top secret, so it's *only* to be used on porting trips." says dad.

"So if Ethan and I are in Paris and there's a problem, how do we call you?" Dad picks up his phone and walks closer.

"Dial 9-1-1-D-A-D on the keypad. That sends an

alert to my sleeve stored in my cabinet which is immediately forwarded to my phone. I put the DAC in and dial 9-1-1-M-A-D to speak to you."

"Does it ring like a phone?" Madison asks.

"No, you'll hear two beeps to let you know there's a call. Then you'll hear me or mom speak."

"And the phone company will never know!" grins Ethan. Madison hugs her dad. "I'm so proud of you, Dad! This is going to be so amazing!"

"Mom and I want you to be prepared for each country and city we visit."

"We're not just going to zip over to France", says mom, "take in a few sights, have something to eat and then teleport to another place. We want you to learn about the cities and countries we visit."

"So many people who live their entire lives and never travel outside their State." says dad. "It's like only ever eating vanilla ice cream, when there's so many incredible places to see."

"So before we teleport, we want you to learn a little about the country, learn some of the language so you can converse a little with the locals, because we won't have our phones to translate." says mom.

"Sure." says Madison, grinning at Ethan.

"The HT is your boarding pass to go anywhere in the world you want." says dad. "By this time next year, you won't believe how much your lives have changed."

"Decide what three countries you'd like to visit next Saturday, then go online and get prepared."

says mom.

"Can't wait!" says Madison, smiling at her very excited brother.

* * *

Three evenings later, Madison and Ethan are on the sofa in the living room, looking at their laptop, as dad walks in.

"How's the research going?" sitting beside Madison. "Great. Do you know how France got its' name? Madison asks. "No."

"Wikipedia says it comes from the Latin word Francia, or realm of the Franks. And the name of the Franks is related to the English word frank, which years ago meant free."

"Huh?" says dad.

"Did you know France is the number one country for tourism?" says Ethan. "They get a hundred million visitors every year! That's two million a week!"

"Really?" says dad. "I know Paris is very popular. What's the population, E?"

"Paris is just over thirteen million .. and France is sixty-eight million."

"You're really into this, that's great!"

"Bonjour, monsieur, comment-vas tu?" says Madison in a French accent.

"Uh, je vais bien, merci, et toi?" grins Ethan.

"Je suis tres bien, merci." grins Madison..

"I'm really impressed, guys! So will Mom."

"We're doing Rio now." says Ethan.

"South America has a hundred million more people than the US." says Madison. "Brazil's its largest country. It covers just under half the land area, and has almost half the population." says Ethan. "It's going to be hard for us to communicate, though." says Madison, reading on her laptop.

"Portuguese in Rio de Janeiro has evolved into its own unique dialect, known as Carioca Portuguese, which has its own set of expressions. This dialect is specific to Rio de Janeiro and is not commonly understood by Portuguese speakers from other parts of Brazil or Portugal."

"Or visitors from Merritt Island, Florida." says Ethan.

"We'll get by." he kisses her cheek. "Love you, sleep well." says Madison as he gets up.

"Hey, listen to this." says Ethan, and he reads,

"English is also widely spoken in Rio de Janeiro, particularly among those in the hospitality industries. Many locals in Rio de Janeiro have learned English in order to communicate with visitors, and English is commonly used in tourist areas and hotels." he grins.

"There you go, we'll be fine." smiles dad.

"I can't wait for Saturday!" grins Madison.

* * *

2. LET'S TELEPORT!

The clock in the Giller's kitchen is showing 6:48 as the family eats breakfast.

"I can't remember the last time you were up before seven on a Saturday." grins mom.

"This isn't a normal Saturday, Mom." grins Madison at Ethan, who has his iPhone out.

"Hey, Siri, what time is it now in Paris, France, please?"

"In Paris, France it's 12:48pm." Siri replies cheerily. "Thanks very much, Siri."

"You're welcome."

"I love how she thanks you." he grins.

"Hey, Siri, what time is it now in Rio de Janeiro, please?" Madison asks.

"It's 7:48am in Rio de Janeiro, Brasilia now."

"We'll be in Paris for the afternoon .. Rio for a second afternoon .. and Waikiki for a third!" Madison grins at Ethan.

"And sleeping in our beds tonight!" says Ethan.

"No luggage .. no security checks! I love it."

"And no jet lag." says Madison.

"I don't want to be carrying all the cash." says

dad, counting several bills. "Here's four hundred for you and E." hands them cash. "Four hundred for you, Laura." hands her cash. "Okay, here's your body neutralizing pill, BNP." taking pills from a small bottle, he hands one to each of them.

"It takes thirty minutes to activate, right?" says Ethan. "Yes, and the affects last how long, Mad'?" asks dad. "Twenty-four hours."

"Right. Always take an extra pill with you in case you're stranded by bad weather. Okay, in the lab in thirty."

Thirty minutes later Madison and Ethan are with Mom and Dad in the basement, all with a cast-sleeve on their arm. "Open your sleeves." dad says. They press the button inside the sleeve and the panel slides open.

"GPS coordinates .. GC's .. are a sequence of long numbers with a few letters. It's very easy to input an incorrect number or letter, so after I landed in error in San Francisco, I created an App that instantly transfers your GC's directly to the keypad in your cast. And our GC's for home are stored so you never have to input them." Madison bites her lower lip, looking excitedly at Ethan, as dad continues.

"Okay, take a deep breath like I demonstrated last night."
Madison and Ethan take a really deep breath and then they force every last ounce they can out of their

lungs.

"Very good … Let's go." Madison and Ethan run upstairs.

A minute later the Giller's are on the backyard deck, checking if any neighbors are outside.

"I think we're good to go, Gordon."

"I'll go first so I'm there when you arrive. Mom will launch after you." Madison and Ethan watch as their Dad takes a deep breath and forcefully expels as much air as he can from his lungs. Then he quickly presses the pound key and … instantly, he's vanished into thin air! Madison and Ethan are in awe looking at mom. "Unbelievable!" they say in unison. "Okay, guys, you see how simple it is?" Madison and Ethan do exactly what they just saw their Dad do, and seconds later Mrs. G. is alone on the deck, smiling proudly.

A minute later Mrs. G. has arrived in Paris and is greeted with excited hugs by her kids in a huge park.

"I can't believe we're really in Paris, Mom!" gushes Madison.

"This is totally insane!" grins her awestruck brother looking around, as mom pulls four wigs from her small backpack and hands two to her kids.

"What are these for?" asks Madison.

"I realized this week we could be in the background when people take photos or videos to post on their social. If someone recognizes us on Instagram or Facebook, how could we explain being in Paris?"

"I could say she's my doppelgänger." grins Madison.

"Your what?" asks Ethan.

"They say everyone has a dead ringer for them." explains Madison.

"That'd be cool meeting my twin." putting on a brown, curly wig.

"You look funny, E!" grins Madison, sporting a long, red wig.

"You look better as a redhead." Ethan chuckles, as Madison playfully sticks out her tongue at him.

"Let's go, guys." says dad, looking different in a black, curly wig. Madison and Ethan choke back giggles as the family walks down the sidewalk, all putting on sunglasses.

Minutes later the Giller's are at the top viewing level of the Eiffel Tower taking in the breathtaking view of Paris.

"That's the Seine River." points out mom, then she reads from a plaque. "It's 18 miles long and empties into the English Channel."

"I read it's so polluted people are advised not to swim in it." says Mad'.

"It scares me when I think what the world could be like when you're as old as Dad and me."

"Let's not rain on the vibe, Mom." says Ethan.

"So, was this Eiffel dude a famous politician?"

"No, it says here he was the architect." says

Madison, reading another plaque. "They began construction in 1887 and finished in 1889."

"Huh, I didn't know they built this high back then." says her brother. "Okay, let's go to the Louvre." suggests mom, as Madison leans in close and whispers. "I hope it's sunny in Rio." They grin.

* * *

The Louvre Museum is on the Right Bank of the Seine, a four minute taxi ride from the Eiffel Tower. It was built in the late 12th Century and houses some of the greatest artworks ever produced. The Giller's are with a small group listening to a Tour Guide who speaks almost reverently.

"Mona Lisa is the most famous artwork in history, painted by Leonardo da Vinci from 1503 and 1519. It depicts Lisa del Giocondo, an Italian noblewoman of the Gherardini family of Florence. The Mona Lisa was owned by French royalty for centuries, and has been displayed in the Louvre since 1797."

"For someone so famous she's not very good-looking." Ethan whispers to Madison, who rolls her eyes. "And why did it take Leo 16 years to paint it?"

"Shhh, E." says Madison.

"Oh, Leo, I look so bland," affecting an Italian woman's voice, "please make me prettier!" Madison stifles a giggle.

Later they're at an outdoor Cafe looking at menus with small photos of each item.

"The Jambon Burr (Beurre) looks good." says Ethan showing mom the selection.

"That's just like a Subway. I want you to try something Parisienne."
Their young waitress walks up. She has a thick, Parisienne accent. "Bonjour." she smiles.

"Bonjour, comment-vas tu?" smiles Madison. The waitress appreciates it.

"Je suis tres bien, merci." grinning. "Have we decided yet?"

"E', the Tartines look delicious!" says Madison showing him the photo.

"Qui, they are very popular. Today we have prosciutto and fig spread, or smoked salmon and capers, on your choice of baguette or sourdough bread."

"I'll have the prosciutto on sourdough, merci beaucoup." grins Ethan. The waitress smiles, appreciating the effort.

"I'll have the smoked salmon and capers on a baguette, s'il vous plait." smiles Madison. The waitress smiles, impressed.

"Two Welshes, s'il vous plait." says mom, and the waitress walks away.

"In two hours we'll be in Rio de Janeiro." whispers Ethan, grinning.

"And in seven hours we'll be in Waikiki having our third afternoon today." grins Madison.

"The rich and famous would be so jealous if they knew." smiles mom.

After lunch the Giller's took a taxi to their next tour -
a one-hour sightseeing cruise along the Seine.
Dozens of tourists are on a double-deck riverboat,
listening to the Tour Guide as they approach Notre
Dame Cathedral.

"Notre Dame Cathedral is dedicated to the
Virgin Mary, and is the most visited monument in
Paris with over twelve million visitors each year.
Construction began in 1163 and was completed
by 1260."
Ethan leans close to Madison and whispers.

"Ninety-seven years!? They sure took their time
in the old days." Madison stifles a giggle.

* * *

A mile more into their cruise, the Tour Guide is
talking about another famous landmark.

"We will be passing under the oldest bridge across
the Seine. Pont Neuf means New Bridge, and the
first stone was laid in May 1578 by Henry the
Third. It was inaugurated by his son, Henry the
Fourth, in 1607. The bridge was a very popular
place with street performers - musicians, jugglers,
fire-eaters - and there were booths along both
sides of the Bridge selling an assortment of
wares."

Ethan looks at Madison. "After four hundred
years I think it's time *New* Bridge got a new name."

"They can't do that, E', there's so much history.

Just imagine what life was like here four hundred
years ago?"

"They weren't thinking about going to Rio de
Janeiro for the afternoon … then snorkelling with
turtles in Waikiki."

"I can't wait! The cruise is almost over!" Madison
grins.

* * *

Prior to their trip Dr. G. had to pre-select the
geographical coordinates (GC's) for the exact
location the family would teleport to in Rio de
Janeiro because they won't have their cell phones.
This required him to be very precise because just one
incorrect digit could have them 'landing' on a busy
street! The photos of the very spacious Paris park he
found online made it an easy selection, and he
downloaded the GC's to the four HT devices. After a
long search Dr. G selected Tijuca National Park in
the mountains overlooking Rio de Janeiro as a good
'landing' destination for the second stop on their
day-long tour. He found many tour companies, and
after a few e-mails using a false name, he'd booked a
two-hour tour. It was only a fifteen minute hike along
a lush, nature trail to reach the small, wooden
structure with the faded sign; Tijuca Park Tours,
where fifty-eight year old Miguel was standing
outside, in dark khakis, long-sleeved shirt and a navy
blue ball cap with the world famous initials 'NY'.

"Uh, lo siento, Miguel?" smiles Dr. G. walking up with the family.

"Si." Miguel smiles. "Senor, Franklin?"

"Si, and my wife, Mrs. Franklin, and our kids." shaking hands.

"Your amigazos no come with you?"

"No, uh, they just dropped us off." smiles Dr. G. "We're really looking forward to this." The family have replaced the wigs with ball caps and shades.

Fifteen minutes later Miguel is leading the Giller's along a narrow, dirt trail carved out by several million footsteps over many centuries. The vegetation is so thick someone hiding ten feet away would be unseen. The steady roar of a waterfall close by requires normal convo to be shouted.

"Tijuca is biggest urban forest in whole world, Señor Franklin."

"Really? How far does it stretch, uh, go?" spreading his arms.

"Forty square kilometers."

"It's incredible to have a park this vast so close to the City. Our big parks are many kilometers away." says Mrs. G.

"Chicago no have parks like this?" Miguel asks. The Giller's shake their heads.

"We read that Tijuca comes from the, is it Tupi?" asks Madison.

"Si." smiles Miguel, impressed. "In Tupi means marsh."

"Mucho marsh." says Ethan, looking around.

"E, look, a capuchin monkey!" Madison points to the little guy sitting on a tree branch thirty feet away, looking at them. "He's so cute!"

"Do they ever go prowling, uh, vamoose …leave here, Miguel?" dad asks.

"No, no." as they walk on.

* * *

A few minutes later they reach a clearing up ahead which provides a spectacular view of Rio de Janeiro far below.

"Oh, wow! What a view mom!" says Madison. The Giller's stand together looking in awe as Miguel looks on.

"Cristo Redentor." says Miguel very respectfully. They look at him. "Jesus The Redeemer." says Mrs. G. "Si." says Miguel.

"How tall, Miguel?" dad asks, raising his right arm high.

"Thirty meters." says Ethan.

"And twenty-eight meters across." says Madison.

"Si." says Miguel, impressed. "You take photo?" he smiles.

"Uh, no, we didn't bring our phones." shrugs dad. "I take photo, e-mail you, Mr. Franklin?" he offers. "Thank you, no." smiles dad, shaking his head, which surprises Miguel.

Later the Giller's are in downtown Rio at an outdoor

cafe enjoying a cold drink.

"So, Mrs. Franklin, did you enjoy the tour?"
Ethan asks.

"Yes, very much. I still can't get over how a huge
rain forest is so close to downtown."

"Yeah, and we must be the only tourists who
didn't take a picture with Jesus The Redeemer
behind them." Madison says.

"It would have been nice, but if he posted it on
his website …?" says dad.

"What's your takeaway so far, Ethan?" mom asks.

"Well, I have a new appreciation for my
geography class now."
Mom, Dad and Madison chuckle.

"I'm sure you do." says mom.

"All these people .. our waitress in Paris, Miguel,
they're living their lives and we're oblivious to
them. It's blowing my mind."

"Yeah, really." says Madison, as Ethan chuckles.

"What, E?"

"Chicago no have parks like this?" he mimics
Miguel. They all grin. "Think how many people he
meets every year from all over the world?" as their
waiter, mid-30's, comes over, smiling.

"Can I take your order, please?"

"Si, uh, the Beirute, could I replace the beef with
more vegetables, por favor?" asks Madison.

"Por sequestro." he smiles, nodding.

"I'll have the same, por favor." says mom.

"Two regular Beirute, por favor." says dad.

"Gracias." he says and walks away.

"You guys will be fluent in so many languages in no time." says mom.

"What are you looking at, Mad'?"

"The clock. Trying to figure out what time it is now in Waikiki." The clock is showing it's 5:30.

"Rio is an hour ahead of us." says Ethan. "And Waikiki is six hours behind us. So it's 10:30 in Waikiki right now."

"Cool. We'll be snorkelling at noon." says Madison. She leans in and whispers. "We'll be the only people in history who've had three afternoons in three countries on the same day." They all grin.

* * *

The Hawaiian islands, including Oahu, were first discovered by British explorer Captain James Cook and fellow Europeans. They initially landed on Kauai, Hawaii's fourth largest island, on Jan. 18, 1778. In Hawaiian language Waikiki means *spouting fresh water* for the springs and streams that fed the wetlands that once separated Waikiki from the interior. Two hundred and fifty-odd years later Waikiki is a top travel destination for tourists from around the world. This afternoon the beaches are crowded with people of all ages enjoying the sunshine and sandy beaches.

A mile from shore the music is lively aboard a two-level, double-hull catamaran with fifty clients enjoying their snorkelling with turtles adventure. Among them are the Giller's who arrived just in time after their 7,443 mile *flight* from Rio de Janeiro that took just **twelve seconds**! They're relaxing in their swim attire, sipping drinks and speaking low.

"This is totally mind-blowing!" marvels Ethan.

"Rebecca and Natalie would be totally freaking!" grins Madison.

"Oh, gosh, they'd be posting everywhere!" says mom.

"Don't worry, they'll *never* know about the HT."

"Anyone hungry?" dad asks.

"No, I had a lovely lunch in Paris, merci." grins Madison in a French accent.

"I have no idea what time it is." chuckles Ethan.

"And the veggie Beirute in Rio was quite filling." says Madison, now sounding like a weary jet-setter, grinning at Ethan, *do you believe this*?

"We have to sample the cuisine of every place we visit." says mom. "When we were here last month we really enjoyed Poke (Po-Kay)." says dad.

"You guys will love it. And you have to try the Shave Ice, Mad'."

"Sounds like a freezie for kids, mom."

"I've never heard of kids' freezie's made with mango, pineapple and melons."

"Really?! I definitely have to try it."

* * *

Three hours later the Giller's are seated at a table for four in Wakani's On The Beach, listening to their Hawaiian waitress.

"Poke is a part of our culture. In Hawaiian it means to slice or cut raw fish crosswise into small pieces. There's many varieties. Do you like sushi?"

"Yeah, most of it." says Madison. "What's the most popular Poke bowl?"

"Shoyu. It's raw tuna, soy sauce, sesame oil, green onions, and sweet onions."

"That's what Dad and I had." looking at the kids. Ethan doesn't look very keen on that. "Do you have cheeseburgers?"

"No, you have to try something local." says mom.

"Do you like shrimp and salmon?" the waitress asks. Ethan gives her a thumbs up. "Love it!"

"Then you'll love our Protein Poke."

"Sounds good, thanks."

"I'll have that as well, please." says Madison.

An hour later lunch is over and Madison and Ethan are chatting with dad.

"Great first Hawaiian meal, dad." says Ethan.

"Yeah, good I have a match on Monday to burn off three lunches." she grins.

"We burned through a lot of cash today, Dad."

"Yes, E', but we had a fantastic day and created some great memories."

Mrs. G walks up quickly, looking unnerved and speaking low.

"We have to leave right now! Wally and Janice Hughes are here!"
Dad's alarmed and stands. He hastily leaves some cash on the table.

"Don't turn around." snaps mom. They walk quickly, as a waitress approaches.

"Sorry, we have to catch our flight!" dad grins. "Cash is on the table … keep the change!" The family doesn't break stride as they reach the front door and rush outside, where they walk quickly to an idling taxi and pile in.

"Hey, how are you today? Where can I take you?" the cabbie asks cheerily.

"Anywhere there's not many people." says dad.

Twenty minutes later the taxi is on a two-lane road with farmland stretching as far as you can see.

"This is perfect, sir." says dad, in the front seat.

The driver is perplexed. "You want to get out *here*, sir?" Dr. G nods. The driver stops on the shoulder of the road. Madison, Ethan and Mom climb out of the back seat, as Dr. G hands the driver some cash. "Uh, do you want me to come back later and get you, sir?"

"No, we'll be fine, thanks." smiles Dr. G as he gets out. "Have a nice day."

"And you, too, sir."
The taxi does a U-turn and as it drives past them,

the driver waves.

"He couldn't understand why we wanted to get out." grins Dr. G. "He asked me if I wanted him to come back later to get us."
Dr. G. looks down the road and confirms the taxi hasn't stopped. "Okay, he's gone. Let's go behind that hay bale." As they walk, "What are the odds Wally and Janice Hughes are here!?" says mom.

"It likely won't be the last time we run into someone we know." says dad.

"For sure." says Ethan. "And next time maybe we won't see them coming."

"That's right." says Madison, as they continue to walk. "So what would you have said if Mrs. Hughes had walked up to our table and surprised you?"

"Uh … hi Janice, hi Wally." says mom.

"Hi, Wally, small world, huh?" grins dad.

"Exactly, how are you, nice to see you." says Madison, as Mom looks at them sheepishly.

"I overreacted, didn't I?"

"It's my fault." says dad. "I'm obsessed with keeping the HT a secret, and never telling our friends about our trips. But you're right, guys, if we run into people we know it's not a big deal."

"But we're not ditching the hats and shades, mom, that's very important." says Madison.

"Oh, yeah, absolutely." says dad.

"Good thing they didn't see us with the wigs on." says Ethan. They laugh loudly as they walk on.

3. BACK HOME

It's almost noon on Sunday and Madison has just started making her fruit smoothies. Her phone rings. '*Bec*' on the screen.

"Hey, 'Bec, what's up?"

"Where'd you get to yesterday? I called like a dozen times?"

"I was out with Mom an' forgot my charger."

"I hate when I do that. So Nat an' me are goin' to the beach to absorb some D. Can you make it?"

"Wish I could, but Mom's here. Can I call you after eight?"

"Sure. Say hi to your mom."

"I will. Have fun. Hi to Nat'."

She puts her phone down and slices open a melon as Mom walks in.

"Mornin' dear, how are you?" hugging her.

"I think this must be what a hangover feels like."

"It is if you feel like I do." yawns mom.

"We traveled just over 25,000 miles you know?"

"It's not the miles .. it's not sleeping for almost 24 hours."

"I was going on adrenaline." pouring mom a cup of coffee.

"Thanks, dear. So, what trip did you like best?"

"Paris was amazing." putting melon in the

blender. "Rio and Waikiki were, too. I think my brain's still trying to make sense of having lunch in three countries on the same day! It's delulu."

"It really is." she sips her coffee. "Imagine all the people around the world you're going to meet." mom smiles.

"It's gonna be wild!" her daughter grins.

* * *

That evening, Madison, Ethan and Dr. G. hug mom on the deck. "Can't wait for our next trip, mom." says Madison.

"Can't wait to hear where you want to go." Dr. G. hugs mom. "Text me when you're home."

"I will." Dr. G. looks around to ensure there's no one looking out windows, as Mrs. G. rolls up her sleeve. "You're good to go, dear."

Mom inhales deeply, then forcefully exhales. She quickly presses the Launch key on the keypad and … she vanishes in a blink! Madison counts out loud -

"3 .. 4 .. 5 .. 6 .. 7 .. 8 .. 9 .. 10 .. 11 .. 12 .. 13 .. 14 .. 15 .. 16 … she's home."

"If the world knew about this, you'd be richer than Elon Musk and Bill Gates combined." says Ethan, grinning at his Dad.

"I know, but the world's just not ready for the HT."

"What do you mean?" Madison asks.

"There's too many bad people who could use it

for the wrong reasons."

"Like what?"

"Someone could commit a robbery or murder someone in Rio and then minutes later they're in Waikiki with a foolproof alibi." Dr. G.'s phone pings. He looks at the screen. It's a text from Mom. He shows them. *Mommy's home* with a heart emoji. He looks at the kids, as if to say, *see what I mean?*

"What if you could make sure criminals could never have it?" asks Madison.

"I can't. Once I file a Patent it becomes public knowledge, so anyone with the money and some smart people could build one."

"If they don't have smart people, they could kidnap you." says Ethan.

"Mom and I discussed that possibility."

"Now you're scaring me, Dad." looking at him. He puts his arm around her as they walk to the door.

"I don't want you worrying, Mad'. I promise you it'll be a long time before the world learns about the HT." as they walk inside.

* * *

The next morning Madison and Ethan are biking to school with Rebecca and Natalie.

"The beach was just overrun with screaming little snotties." says Rebecca. "Marco Polo." she says sing-songy. "It's soooo annoying!

"What'd you do yesterday, Mad'?" asks Natalie.

Madison looks at Ethan, who's yawning. *We went to Paris for lunch. Then hopped down to Rio for a few hours and then zipped over to Waikiki.*

"We visited my aunt and uncle. Boring. How's your knee" getting the convo away from her..

"Good. I iced it pretty much all day Saturday."

"Don't push it today." Madison cautions.

"I won't."

*　*　*

That afternoon, the *Rebels* are playing Conference rival Lakefield. The game is tied 2-2 with three minutes left in regular time. Madison scored the game's first goal on a superb individual effort, before Lakefield tied it just a minute prior to halftime. In the seventy-second minute Madison set up Rebecca with a deft pass and she buried it past the sprawling keeper to give the *Rebels* the lead. But seven minutes later Lakefield tied it again, and neither Team has had a sniff at a scoring opportunity since. During an injury timeout, *Rebels* Coach Cindy Jamieson discusses strategy with her charges leaning in.

"They're running on fumes, guys! Time for that extra gear!" The eleven tired, sweaty girls clasp hands and shout in unison, "Rebels!" As Madison and Rebecca walk on the field, Madison leans close.

"Crosby's favoring her left ankle. Let's exploit it." Rebecca nods. These are the moments Madison embraces. The game on the line. She loves how it makes her feel. Knowing her teammates are looking to her to inspire them. Many athletes wilt under the pressure at key moments. Taking a penalty kick in a tie game with one minute left. The fear of failure feels like a 100 pound weight on their chest. *I don't want to look bad.* Their nerves *rule them.* But it wasn't always so for Madison. She had allowed her eight year old nerves to rule her one too many times. Then Mom told her about *visualization.* How she needed to really imagine herself in pressure spots while laying in her darkened bedroom. Create those moments where she could feel her body tense up. Her heart racing. Nerves overwhelming her. So when she was next in that moment in a real game, she'd been there a hundred times. It became a 20-minute ritual every morning for her during her ninth Winter. When the new season arrived, Madison was fearless, and her game soared to new heights. The goals piled up and Dr. G. had to buy another bookcase to display her MVP and All Star trophies. Now in her Junior year, scouts from the nation's top Soccer programs are attending Madison's games and taking video home to show their coaching staff. Watching from the stands with the hundred or so *Rebels* students and Faculty, Ethan's with his dad and his friend Garret.

"Mad's gonna score, I can feel it." says Ethan Minutes later the scoreboard shows it's still 2-2, and the timer is clicking down the seconds, now at only thirty-seven. Madison steals the ball from a defender at mid-field. She chips a deft pass to Rebecca, and puts on a burst of speed to surge past a defender.

Rebecca instinctively reads the play and slides a slick, leading pass for Madison as she breezes past a defender favoring her left ankle. Madison's on a clear break! When she's fifteen feet from the keeper Madison executes a clever stutter-step-fake. The keeper bites, and Madison cooly slides the winning strike into the gaping goal! Her teammates rush to congratulate her on her Ronaldo-like play.

In the stands, Ethan hi-5's his dad and Garret.

"What'd I tell you!"

"That was spectacular!" says Garret.

"Mad's always so cool under pressure." says Dr. G. "She be a great astronaut." looking proudly at her with her happy teammates.

"She can do anything she wants." says Ethan proudly.

* * *

After dinner Madison, Ethan and Dr. G. are Face-Timing with Mrs. G.

"And then she did this move .. what do you call it?" Ethan asks her.

"Stutter-step." enjoying his effort.

"Right, and the goalie, I mean the keeper, she totally went for it." trying to mimic Madison's clever move and the keeper's flailing effort. "And Mad' just kicked it past her. It was amazing!"

"I'll make sure his phone's charged for her next game." says dad.

"Match." corrects Madison, smiling at her dad,

who shrugs.

"So have you guys decided where we're going next?"

"Thinking about Australia." says Ethan.

"Great!"

"Okay, we gotta head out now." says Ethan.

"Good luck, dear."

"The votes are already in, mom" he shrugs.

"Call me when you get back."

"Yup." and the screen goes blank.

* * *

The Walker High auditorium is packed with students and parents for the Science Awards presentation. Madison and Dr. G. are seated in the fourth row with Ethan and Garret, looking at Mr. Godfrey addressing the throng.

"The diversity of projects undertaken by our students this year was really quite remarkable. It made it very challenging to determine who was most deserving to receive the Gold Cup. However, after much debate, our Committee voted for the team of Ethan Giller and Garret Hughes and their Drone Bird."

The audience applauds loudly as Ethan and Garret stand up, very excited. Madison hugs Ethan.

"Way to go, E! I'm so proud of you!"

"Thanks, Mad."

"Great job, Garret!" she hugs him, as Dr. G. hugs

Ethan.

"I'm very proud of you, Ethan."

"Thanks for all your help, Dad."

Ethan and Garret make their way towards the stage, accepting handshakes from several classmates on the way. Madison's filming it on her phone as Ethan and Garret accept their trophy from Mr. Godfrey. The applause subsides, and Ethan shyly speaks into the microphone.

"Thank you, Mr. Godfrey, and the Committee. Uh, there were a lot of great projects this year and, uh, Garret and I worked really hard on our Drone Bird. Uh, I wanna thank my Dad for all the support he's given me over the years. He's my hero and, uh, there's a lotta pressure when your Dad's a legend like he is, so it's pretty cool to make you proud, Dad."

The audience applauds. Dr. G. is moved as Madison smiles at him.

Mr. Godfrey steps to the microphone.

"Garret, tell us a little about your Drone Bird."

"Okay, so, uh, Ethan came up with the idea of designing a drone that looks and flies like a small bird, but it also has a small video camera in its mouth so it can record stuff, you know?"

"Very clever. Ethan, what's the range and how long can it go between charges?"

"So the range is 300 feet, give or take, and, uh, it can remain in the air for about eleven minutes before it needs to be charged."

"That's very impressive. Ladies and gentlemen,

our winners of the Gold Cup, Ethan Giller and Garret Hughes." says Mr. Godfrey, to loud applause.

* * *

An hour later in her Palo Alto condo, Mrs. G. is proudly watching Madison's video on her laptop of Ethan speaking tonight.

" … it can remain in the air about eleven minutes before it needs to be charged."

"That's very impressive. Ladies and gentlemen, our winners of the Gold Cup, Ethan Giller and Garret Hughes."
Mom closes her laptop and smiles into her phone, where Ethan is grinning.

"I'm so proud of you, Ethan. I wish I could have been there."

"Thanks, Mom."
Madison pops on screen, smiling over her brother's left shoulder. "Great speech, huh? Right off the cuff." "Yes, and very humble. Just like his Dad."
Dr. G. pops on screen over Ethan's right shoulder.

"Got me a little choked up, Laura."

"Me too. We'll find a great restaurant in Australia to celebrate your win!"

"Great! We'll call you Friday evening. We have to get back to our research. Love you."
They all blow kisses and the screen goes blank.

"How's the research going?"

"We're almost finished." Madison says.

"What have you learned?"

"The name Australia is derived from the Latin Terra Australis, which means southern land." Ethan says. "And it's the world's smallest continent."

"What's the population?"

"Twenty-seven million." Madison says.

"Melbourne is the capital city, right?"

"No, we thought it was, too. It's Canberra. Only half a million live there, and Melbourne has five million, go figure."

"They have some great expressions, Dad." says Ethan, looking at the laptop.

"*She'll be apples* means everything will be alright. *Defo, d-e-f-o-* means definitely, but *devo, d-e-v-o* means devastated."

"We'll have to be careful how we say that." dad grins.

"And a very good friend is a *robber*." says Madison.

"Huh? Saying you can't have too many robbers wouldn't go over well here."

"Defo." says Madison. "How's your research going?"

"I watched a lot of YouTube videos and mapped out where to go, safe places to port, and logged the GC's into our HT's. It's gonna be a great day."

"Where are some of the places we're going? asks Ethan.

"I'm going to surprise you."

"Please, no museums." says Madison.

"Yeah, defo." grins Ethan.

"I promise. Don't be up late, guys." he kisses Madison on the cheek.

"We won't. Sleep well."

"It's still hard to believe we can go anywhere we want." says Ethan.

"Remember how excited we'd be going to Fort Lauderdale for a weekend?"

"Yeah, it's crazy."

"E', we're going to Australia on Saturday *for the day*!"

"Actually we'll be there on Sunday."

"Right, and we'll be back home on Saturday night." she chuckles.

"And enjoy a second Sunday this weekend!" he laughs.

"Can't wait!" she grins.

Dad watches from the hallway, enjoying their excitement.

* * *

4. G'DAY MATE!

It's Saturday morning and the Sun is just coming up.
The Giller's are on the back deck, seconds away
from their next teleporting adventure. Dad is taking
a deep breath and then he forcefully exhales as much
air as he possibly can. He quickly taps the Launch
key on his HT keypad and a second later … he's
gone! "See you in Australia, mom." grins Madison as
she breathes in deeply.

In 1770, James Cook claimed possession of the east
coast of Australia on behalf of Britain to pre-empt
the French colonial empire from expanding there.
Britain was experiencing massive overcrowding of
their prisons and selected Australia to serve as a
penal colony. On January 20, 1788, a fleet of eleven
convict ships docked in Botany Bay in Sydney, New
South Wales, which was the first European
settlement on the continent. Until the early 19th
century, Australia was best known as New Holland, a
name first applied by the Dutch explorer Abel
Tasman in 1644 as Nieuw Holland. The explorer
Matthew Flinders is credited with being responsible

for *Australia* being popularized, as he believed it was '*more pleasing to the ear,*' and was '*an assimilation to the names of the other great portions of the Earth.*'

* * *

While Madison and Ethan were poring through Wikipedia's pages to learn about Australia, Dr. G was tasked with the responsibility of pre-selecting a safe location to land in Melbourne. This meant ensuring there were no big rock formations, roads with moving vehicles and bodies of water within miles. He selected Fitzroy Gardens, one of the cities most popular destinations, where the Giller's arrived safely, a minute apart.

"It's really beautiful." Madison says, looking around.

"Great weather for us." says mom, as they put on their ball caps.

"A minute ago it was seven o'clock Saturday morning," says Ethan, "and here it's Sunday morning just after nine o'clock. We lost our Saturday."

"No, you didn't." says dad. "You're spending your Saturday in Melbourne, and tomorrow you'll have a *second* Sunday this weekend. Okay, I've planned a fourteen hour day for us starting with one of the top-rated beaches in Melbourne, PortSea Front Beach. It's only fifteen minutes away, and we're getting there on the city's free tram."

"Cuttin' costs, Dad?" asks Ethan.

"We don't have our credit cards so we can't Uber. And I want us to get a feel for the city, experience the culture."

"Cool, let's get started." says Madison.

A few minutes later the Giller's are boarding the Tram.

"G-Day, mate!" Ethan grins to the male driver, 40's.

"G'Day, mate." he smiles as the Giller's take seats up front just off to the driver's right. The Tram is two connected streetcars that look like they were built fifty years ago, each with maybe 30 seats, but spotlessly clean and bright.

"It goes right through the downtown core." says dad.

"First time down under?" asks the driver, waiting on a red light.

"Yes. We're going to PortSea Front Beach for the morning."

"She'll be apples." he smiles as the light turns green and he turns away.

"She'll be apples." Ethan whispers to Madison, both grinning.

PortSea Front Beach has an L-shaped pier that juts about two hundred feet out and a hundred and thirty feet on the 'L'. The beach itself is quite narrow, and right behind it is a large Beer Garden where the Giller's are seated for lunch after their relaxing morning on the beach.

"G'Day, I'm Hilda, enjoyin' the arvo?" she smiles.

"Arvo is afternoon, mom." explains Ethan.

"Oh, yes, we are, thanks." smiling at Hilda.

"What are your most popular lunches?"

"Do ya like fish?"

"Yes, we do."

"You'll love our Barramundi. Grilled, or fried. Do you like beef, or pork?"

"Yes." dad says.

"We do barbecued snags topped with your choice of spices and sauces. Chico rolls are dough filled with beef, cabbage, onions and carrots. And of course, grilled Kangaroo's a fave." she smiles. Madison and mom flinch hearing this last fave.

"Hilda, do you have vegetarian?" Madison asks.

"Ya, the Witchery Grub, it's a large wood-eating larva of a moth that's packed with protein."

Madison grimaces. "I'll have the Barramundi, please .. grilled."

"I'll have the same, Hilda." says mom.

"I'm gonna give those Chico rolls a shot, Hilda." says Ethan.

"I'll have the barbecued snags, please .. beef." says dad. Hilda writes it down. "To drink?"

"Two beers." says dad.

"Iced tea, please." says Madison.

"Coke, no ice, please." says Ethan. Hilda walks away and Madison leans forward and speaks low.

"*Large wood-eating larva of a moth*? I didn't want to know any more about it." making a *Ewww* face.

"There's a rich Aboriginal history here, Mad'. A lot of their favorite food goes back hundred's of years."

"When we get home I'm Googling large wood-eating larva of a moth." says Ethan.

"I defo don't want to know what you find."

"*Defo?*" asks mom, puzzled.

"It's Aussie short for definitely." says Ethan.

"D-e-f-o."

"But you need to enunciate clearly because devo - d-e-v-o means devastated." adds dad.

"We've only been here four hours and I've learned a lot." says mom. "How could anyone eat a grilled kangaroo? They're so adorable."

"They look adorable, but they're got a mean streak. You should see them fighting each other. I saw a video on YouTube, throwing punches with their little arms, and kicking, it was too funny."

"I'm glad we're staying here all day." says Madison, lowering her voice and leaning in. "Doing Paris, Rio and Waikiki in one day was really hectic."

"Yeah, but very cool." says Ethan.

"I agree, Mad'." says mom. "We don't have to rush our lunch and then we'll see what Dad's got planned for us next." smiling at him.

"You're going to love it." he grins.

* * *

Ninety minutes later the Giller's are among a few dozen tourists and locals on board the Puffing Billy Railway as its' eight cars chug away from Belgrave Station.

"This is like stepping into a time-warp!" grins Mrs. G.

"Yeah, it's been operating since the year 1900."

"Amazing!" says Ethan.

"Where are we going, Dad?" Madison asks.

"It's an hour's ride through the rural areas. I thought it'd be a fun way to see the outskirts."

An elderly man and woman are seated opposite.

"She ran from Upper Ferntree Gully station back when my great-grand-pappy was a wee ankle biter."

"Really? So she's had a few million passengers." says dad.

"She begun haulin' timber from the farms." old Aussie says. "First time in these parts?"

"Yes." smiles dad.

"Uh, sir, have you ever had a Witchery Grub?" Ethan asks.

The old man's eyes light up a little. "Crikey, they're gnarly! A robber does the best ya ever tasted!" as the woman with him grins and nods.

Mrs. G and Madison look blankly.

"Canadian?" gesturing towards Dr. G.

"No, US ... uh, St. Louis."

"California?" Aussie says, brow furrowed.

"No, Missouri."

From his blank look, old Aussie has never heard of *The Show Me State*.

The Puffing Billy maintained a maximum speed of fifteen miles per hour as it crawled through the rural areas. When it reached the end of the line many of the passengers stayed on for the return trip. That wasn't in Dr. G.'s afternoon agenda, and walking along the platform Madison has a question for her brother.

"Why'd you ask him about that thing I'm never saying again?!"

"Hilda said they're really popular .. just checking."

"Did you understand what he said about them?" mom asks.

"Yeah, crikey means amazing." says Ethan, grinning. "And robber is slang for best friend."

"Really? Do I want to know what wee ankle biter is?"

"That's what they call little kids here." grins Ethan.

"Oh, my gosh!" mom grimaces.

"Other than that, how'd you like Puffing Billy? asks dad.

"It was a very good choice, dear."

"Yeah, it was, dad." says Madison.

"Good. Alright, we have to go over behind the parking lot."

"Where are we porting to?" Madison asks.

"We're going to do something not even Mom and I have done." he smiles, as they look at him, intrigued.

* * *

The Yarra River flows from East-Central Victoria through downtown Melbourne. This evening a luxury one hundred foot, double-deck ship is slowly cruising its still waters, providing a spectacular backdrop for its' eighty diners enjoying a meal under the stars. The Giller's are seated, reading the menus.

"This is so beautiful, Gordon."

"Yeah, even though we're a little under-dressed." says Madison.

"Don't worry about it, Mad', it's Australia." says Ethan. "Mom, did you know England shipped thousands of convicts here three hundred years ago?"

"No. Why?"

"Their prisons were overcrowded."

"And Australia had become a Commonwealth under England." says Madison.

"Did you learn this in geography?"

"No, doing our research for the trip."

"I'm impressed! "

"What's everyone having?" asks dad.

"The quinoa avocado salad." says Madison.

"Ya gotta say avo salad." grins Ethan.

"Right."

"What are you having, E?" asks mom.

"Since I can't have the barbecue chicken wings with blue cheese, or the mini man burgers, or the sticky chicken winglets, I'm going with the Potato Frittata."

"Oh, my gosh, they have grilled kangaroo with Australian native fruits."

"Lucky you saw it before you ordered, Mad'." Ethan grins, as their better dressed waitress, late 20's, crisp, white blouse and black slacks, walks up.

"How's the serenity?" she smiles.

"Hi, yes, it is very serene." smiles mom.

"How's the serenity means good evening." says Ethan.

"Oh, well it is very serene, too."

"I'm Kyrie, yer server."

"What a lovely name." says mom.

"Thanks."

"Kyrie, the river's really narrow … how far does it go like this?" Ethan asks.

"Everyone wants to know." she smiles. "It's two hundred and forty-two kilometers long, startin' in Victoria. An' it hardly gets wider than what you see, 'bout fifty meters .. a few spots it gets to three hundred fer a bit. So, uh, have you decided yet?"

"Yes, we have …." says Dad.

* * *

Two hours later the Giller's are working on the last of their desserts as Madison leans close and whispers. "Thanks for a really great day, Dad."

50

"Yeah, very awesome, Dad."

"You put a lot of effort into making it very special, Gordon."

"I'm very happy you enjoyed it."

"It's still hard to believe we'll be sleeping in our beds tonight." say Ethan.

"Sure beats a twenty-hour flight." says Madison. She's barely got the words out when it suddenly starts to rain hard, crashing the Giller's lighthearted mood as they realize *they can't port home now*!

"Kyrie?!" dad calls out, forcing a half-smile, as she comes over.

"What can I getcha, Mr. Willoughby?"

"Uh, we left our phones at the hotel. Could I use your's, please? I need to check something."

"Of course." opening her phone for him. "Take yer time." She walks off. Madison and Ethan lean in close.

"What are you doing, Dad?" whispers Madison.

"Checking the weather." typing. "May not be raining close by and we can take a train or bus."

"And it was so beautiful all day." says mom.

"Okay, it's not raining in Healesville, and the storm's not going in their direction. Siri, how far is Healesville, Australia from Melbourne, Australia, please."

"Here's what I found on the web." Siri says cheerily. Dad reads, "It's forty miles away … let's check the trains." as Kyrie walks up.

"Find what ya needed?"

"Is there a train or bus to Healesville tonight?"

"No, not 'til mornin'." handing them their bill.

"Oh, okay, thanks. Appreciate it." he hands her the phone and she walks off.

"Gordon, there's no guarantee it won't be raining in Healesville. I think we should find a motel and get some sleep. It's nine-thirty, so do the math, E'."

"Okay, that means it's seven thirty Sunday evening at home, which gives us twelve hours to get home .. and it's four-thirty in the afternoon in Palo Alto."

"So we get up in six hours." mom says. "If it's not raining, we port home. If it is, we catch a train, or bus, or taxi to where it isn't raining."

* * *

At six-thirty on Tuesday morning the Giller's awoke to the sound of the rain beating down on their motel roof five miles outside Melbourne. It was four-thirty on Monday morning in Merritt Island, so they took a taxi to the train station and boarded one a lot faster than Puffing Billy that was heading thirty miles east where the ticket seller had assured them it would be sunny. It was. It was the first time they had teleported so close to the twenty-four hour limit for one Body Neutralizing Pill (BNP), so they each took their backup, just to be safe. Then they hurried to a secluded spot behind the Wesler Commuter rail station and hugged mom goodbye.

"We'll never forget this trip." chuckles dad.

"It was amazing!" says mom.

"You mean it was crikey!" grins Ethan.

They all laugh. After another hug, they each breathe in deeply …

* * *

5. MEETING RAFAEL

At the *Rebels* practice that afternoon Coach Jamieson couldn't help but notice her star Striker didn't have her usual energy.

"Didn't pound nine last night, Mad'?"
No, the beds in our Melbourne motel sucked, Coach.

"Barely got five."

"How come?"
It was raining and we couldn't teleport home.

"Just one of those nights. I'll be catchin' up tonight, Coach."

When Madison got home Ethan and Dr. G are on a video call with Mom.

"Mad's here." says dad, holding the phone for mom to see her.

"Hi, dear, how are you?"

"Exhausted. You?" sitting beside dad.

"Good. I got another four hours of zzzz's which really helped."

"Lucky you. I need a dozen tonight."

"I was just saying how nice it was to be there for the whole day."

"And from now on I'll be checking the weather

forecast the day before we port." says dad. "If it looks bad, I'll have a backup plan."

"You guys are going to love Majorca."

"Can't wait, but right now I just need food and zzzz's." she yawns.

* * *

Madison got caught up on her zzzz's and was in fine form on Friday afternoon scoring two more goals in the *Rebels* 3-1 win. She and Ethan managed to learn a lot about Spain and Majorca, which is six hours ahead of Merritt Island. That required the Giller's to hit the pillows at nine o'clock on Friday night so they could get up at four o'clock Saturday morning, when it was ten o'clock in Majorca. Upon their arrival they taxied two miles away to board the '*Samba*' for a four-hour cruise with great food and music. The ship dropped anchor a mile from shore and Madison and Ethan went snorkelling for the second time. Then a great buffet was served with lively music.

"This looks good." says Madison, looking at a large serving bowl.

"Yes, Tumbet Mallorquin," says the late 20's female Server. "Vegetables gently fried in extra virgin olive oil and then it is baked. Much like ratatouille or Spanish pisto."

"I'd like that, please." Madison says.

"I will, too." says mom.

Dr. G and Ethan opted for the roasted pork cheek with mushrooms and onions, and they sat at a table sheltered from the Sun to enjoy their lunch.

"The water was so clear, I could see for a hundred yards!" says mom. "And there's so many fish! Green, yellow, red, blue .. big, small!"

"We're defo doin' more snorkelling trips." Madison says.

"Defo." says Ethan taking a big bite of the roasted pork.

"Oh, defo for sure!" mom says, smiling at dad. He's really happy seeing his family's joy. "To another great day!" raising his glass. They clink glasses.

* * *

After the '*Samba*' docked the Giller's relaxed on the beach for two hours. It was only eleven o'clock in the morning on their Merritt Island circadian 'clock', and they were looking forward to having dinner in downtown Palma, the largest city of the Balearic Islands with a population of just over four hundred thousand.

It was eight o'clock when the Giller's arrived by taxi in downtown Palma. The street is alive with music as people enjoy a meal and drinks at the outdoor Cafes on each side. "We defo look like tourists." says Madison, as they put on their ball caps. Dr. G is looking up. "There's several CCTV cams .. let's eat inside." Dad and mom are walking just ahead of the kids, and they've only walked a short distance when a young guy, late teens, rushes up and grabs Madison's backpack and runs off.

"Hey! He stole my bag! Someone stop him!" Madison yells.

Two hundred feet ahead a strapping young man, maybe18, in jeans and t-shirt, has heard Madison's call for help and gives chase. He knocks the thief down and restrains him as a Police Officer rushes up and takes over. The Giller's rush up to the handsome hero, his black hair in a ponytail.

"Thank you so much!" Madison says.

"It was nothing." he shrugs modestly. "We don't like it when nice people come to our country and punks ruin their trip."

"You were very brave, thank you." says Mrs. G.

"I recently completed my nine month training with the Police Academy. Uh, I'm Rafael .. Garcia."

"Hi .. Madison, my brother Ethan, and my Mom and Dad." They shake hands.

"So will this be your first arrest, Rafael?" Dr. G asks.

"No, I'm in my fourth month of specialized training."

"Rafael, can we buy you a drink as a thank you?" asks mom.

"Thank you, ma'am. I don't drink alcohol, but a soda would be nice."

Drinks turned into dinner at a restaurant. Madison is seated beside mom, opposite Rafael, who's between Dr. G and Ethan. On the table is a large pan of delicious-looking Paella that's already half-eaten.

"There's many different types of paella. My grandfather says the original goes back to the 1800's in Valencia where he was born, about 160 miles from here. It was a way to feed a lot of people and for families to enjoy food together."

"What does paella mean, Rafael?" Madison asks.

"It comes from the Latin word *patella* which is for the pan it's cooked in."

"Huh, patella in English is a tendon in the knee." says Madison.

"Really?" he grins. "There's actually another theory the name comes from the Arabic word for leftovers."

"Best leftovers I've ever had." grins Ethan.

"Yes, but the leftovers could be duck, chicken, rabbit, rice and tomatoes. A perfectly-cooked paella has a layer of toasted rice on the bottom of the pan called the *socarrat*, which in English means singed, but not burned."
It's clear he knows his way around cuisine, which impresses Madison and mom.

"It's delicious." says Madison.

"Did you learn this from your mom?" mom asks.

"No." his smile diminishes. "I was only seven when she passed. She had cancer. But yes, she made a great paella." the smile returns at the nice memory.

"I'm so sorry, Rafael." says Madison sincerely.

"Thank you. But it's all good. I'm very fortunate, I have a great papa and some good friends."

"What does your Papa do?" Dr. G. asks.

"He's a very good mechanic. Cars, trucks, boats. Until eighteen months ago I was going to follow in his steps. Then I met a gentleman with the Police Force at a Judo competition I was in." he smiles, "and here I am."

"Wait, what happened?" Dr. G grins.

"I won the competition and the gentleman told me the Police Force is always looking for young men and women with special skills, and would I be interested in doing an interview. I talked with papa, and we agreed I should. It went well, and then I scored well in their written test and they offered me the nine-month training."

"You're a very modest young man, Rafael." says mom.

He shrugs. "Papa told me as a young boy, nunca toques tu propia bocina … never blow your own horn."

"Your Papa sounds like a very good man." says Dr. G. "He must be very proud of you." mom says, very impressed.

"Thank you, yes, he is a great man."

"Have you ever been to America?" asks Madison.

"No, but I'd like to some day. Florida sounds a lot like Majorca, being so close to the ocean."

"Dad works for NASA, the Space Agency?"

Ethan says. Mom shoots a look at Dr. G., as if to say so much for being anonymous.

"Really?" Rafael is impressed.

"And Madison's captain of her school soccer team." says Mrs. G., trying to get the focus away from Dad.

"Impressive! Do you play soccer, too, Ethan?"

"I don't play sports. I like watching Mad's games, but my passion's science."

"Oh, man, I'm so bad in science." grinning. "So is it your first time here?"

"Theirs'. My wife and I were here, uh, once."

"How long are you here for?"

"We're flying home … shortly" says Mrs. G. Rafael's disappointment is obvious.

"Oh, how long have you been here?"

"Not long enough! There's so much we want to see." says Madison.

"You should give us your number so we can hear how your training is going." suggests Mrs. G.

"Sure." smiles Rafael. "I can put my number in your phone, Madison."

"Actually, we, uh, we left our phones at the hotel."

"Yeah, those roaming charges can really add up." adds mom quickly.

"Of course. Okay, I'll get a pen and paper." he walks off.

"So much for keeping a low profile." says Dr. G.

"No worries. He's a good guy." says mom.

"Any guy that can fix car engines is a cool guy." says Ethan.

Rafael comes back and sits down. He writes on a piece of paper and hands it to Madison. "My cell .. I don't do social."

"Oh, okay, I'll shoot you mine later."

"Thanks again for rescuing Mad's backpack." says Mrs. G.

"Thanks for the nice dinner. It was a real pleasure to meet you. It's too bad you're leaving tomorrow."

"Rafael, if the Police should ask you for any information about us, I'd really appreciate it if you could keep our identity secret." says Dr. G. "The thief's father or uncle could be criminals, you never know, right?" he shrugs.

"And we wouldn't want to have to come back for a trial." adds Mrs. G.

"I understand. Don't worry, I'll handle it, sir."

"I appreciate it, Rafael."

Later the Giller's are walking down the alley where they arrived.

"Handsome, talented and humble!" says Mrs. G.

"Not many like him back home." says Madison.

"Good he doesn't do social."

"We'll never forget this trip, guys." says mom.

"Hope it's the only time we have to deal with the

Police." says Madison, as they look around to make sure they're not being observed by anyone.

* * *

The next day the Giller's are in the living room.

"We've been to Paris .. Rio de Janeiro .. Waikiki .. Melbourne .. and Majorca." says dad. "Have a favorite, Mad'?"

"Paris was great, but when we go there next I'd like to go into the rural areas. The Rio tour was amazing .. I wanna go back for sure. I defo wanna see the Great Barrier Reef .. but I'd say Waikiki and Majorca are my faves .. the beaches .. the snorkelling. What's your fave, E'?"

"Waikiki and Majorca. I could snorkel and eat Paella and Poke every day."

"With the HT you can." says dad. "What's your fave, Laura?"

"I don't have just *one*. I'm just so grateful we've had these amazing trips. Seeing you guys so excited .. I've really missed us being together as a family, and … I'm getting emotional … I feel so grateful .. we're so blessed." Madison gives her a hug. "We are, mom. And we're gonna have a lot more amazing trips .. wherever and whenever we want!"

* * *

Rafael has been summoned to the Palma Police Station to complete his statement on the theft of Madison's backpack. He's sitting opposite Officer Raol Herrera.

"Her father said because the backpack was returned, he preferred to remain anonymous."

"Did he say why?"

"He was concerned the kid's family might have connections, you know?"

"He thinks the Mafia's gonna come after his family over this?"

"I know." Rafael shakes his head.

"You did good, Raf. The Chief was very impressed."

"Thanks, Raol."

"It's going to look good on your final report. How many months left?"

"Five."

That evening Rafael is helping his papa work on a car engine in his garage. They work fast swapping out parts, replacing an air filter.

"The guy's my age. His papa's in prison and his mama lost her job. He saw them and figured they're wealthy Americans, he might get some cash."

"He can make cash working." closing the car hood. "Anyway, you did good. You helped these people, I'm proud of you."

"Thanks, papa."

"My work is done for the day. Now we eat." he walks with his son.

Rafael and his papa live in a small bungalow a hundred meters from the ocean. Inside their modestly furnished, seven hundred square feet, two bedroom home, they've cleaned up and are enjoying a nice dinner of pasta, shrimp, broccoli and tomatoes.

"You work too many hours, papa."

"You know I enjoy my work."

"Yes, but there's many other things to enjoy."

"In four years I will make the last payment to the Bank, so you will always have a home. Then I will have time to enjoy." raising his wine glass.

"You could have many happy days in those four years, papa."

"Yes, but then my last payment to the Bank will be in six years."

Rafael looks towards the wall where a large portrait of his beautiful mother, posing with a smiling, seven year old Rafael and his papa, hangs prominently.

* * *

Friday evening Madison, Ethan and Dr. G are enjoying a barbecue on the deck.

"She won a competition last year against the top one hundred computer programmers in India."

"Very impressive." says Madison.

"At seventeen?" says Ethan. "What's her I.Q?"

"I believe it's 159."

"Nipping at your heels, Dad." says Madison, as she re-fills his iced tea. "What's her name?"

"Maya."

"Why are you going?" asks Ethan.

"I've been consulting with them on their Space program for many years. They're way behind us, but they've moved closer to Europe and Russia's programs. They want me to meet Maya."

"How long will you be away?" asks Ethan.

"A week."

"What city are you going to?" asks Madison.

"Mumbai." he sips his iced tea. "Hey, maybe you guys and mom can zip in for a day."

"I've always wanted to go to India." says Madison. "E?" looking at him.

"It's not on my top ten, but I hear the air fare's cheap." he grins.

Madison's phone rings. She picks it up. *Rafael* on the screen. "Hey, Rafael! Great timing, we just finished dinner."

"Hey everyone! So I have good news. The guy pleaded guilty to stealing your bag, so you don't need you to testify or file a statement."

Madison sneaks a look at her dad and brother. *That's really good news.*

"That's great, Rafael." says Dr. G. "I really appreciate your help in this."

"Of course, sir. They gave me a commendation, which helps me."

"That's great! You deserve it." says Madison.

"Good for you." says dad.

"Thanks very much."

"How's your training going?" Dad asks.

"Very good, thanks. Every day is different. Today was learning procedural duties, filing reports, and in the afternoon we had instructors teach us how to handle high-speed car chases."

"That sounds exciting." says Ethan.

"It was. We went to a race track and they had the course set up where we had to react quickly to a cardboard cut-out of a person that would suddenly appear and we had to swerve to not hit it."

"How fast were you going?" Madison asks.

"Over a hundred kilometers, nothing crazy." Rafael reacts and looks away.

"Oh, I'm sorry, papa needs my help. I'll call you in a few days."

"Okay, bye Rafael." they say and wave as the call ends.

"He's a fine young man. His mother would be very proud." says dad.

"Yeah, she would." says Madison.

6. THE CONNECTION

Gordon Giller was the only child of Walter Giller, an esteemed Professor of Mathematics at Massachusetts Institute of Technology. Walter realized his son had a special gift when Gordon was doing eighth grade math at the age of five. Walter immediately enrolled his son in a Mensa school where he'd be educated alongside other smart children. Gordon was soon fascinated by space travel and read every book about America's race to land the first man on the Moon. His ability to learn about the physical affects of extended space travel on astronauts led to him starting university at age twelve, to study molecular physics. When he graduated at seventeen he had many job offers from America's top companies, including one from NASA, where he'd always dreamed of working.

At the age of twenty-three, Gordon met Laura Edmonds, a pretty brunette who was beginning her career working as an assistant to a municipal politician with a keen interest in preserving Florida's natural resources. They were married two years later, and welcomed Madison and Ethan within three

years. Gordon quickly rose through the ranks at
NASA, while Laura took online courses to earn her
teaching Certificate, specializing in Environmental
Studies. She taught at the Community College for
ten years, and when the kids were 14 and 13, Laura
received an offer from Stanford University to join
their Faculty as an Associate Professor. Gordon
couldn't move to Palo Alto, but he knew this was an
opportunity Laura couldn't pass up. It's been a
challenge for them, adjusting to not having Mom at
home, but as Dr. G's plane was in final prep to land
at Mumbai's largest airport, he knew if Laura hadn't
accepted the Stanford position, he likely would not
have spent the past two years developing the HT.

It's the crowning achievement of his incredible
career, despite the fact he hopes the world will not
learn of it until after his death. Of course he had no
way of knowing that his trip to Mumbai to meet a
very talented seventeen year old girl will be the
beginning of a friendship with his daughter and son
and their new friend, Rafael. Or that this friendship
will soon develop into an extraordinary partnership
that will eventually create a global media obsession
to learn the identities of these four, amazing
teenagers.

Viraj Patel is the Director of India's Space
Research Organization (ISRO) Department of
Space (DoS), which has the world's largest
constellation of remote-sensing satellites and has sent

three missions to the Moon and one to Mars. Dr. G. has done many Zoom meetings with Viraj, and today they are meeting in person for this first time.

"Gordon, it is so good to meet you after our many Zooms." in the limousine driving from the airport.

"Thank you, Viraj. It's wonderful to meet you. I was delighted to receive your invitation."

"We're very honored to have you. We appreciate you making such a long trip, but we're quite sure you will be most impressed with young Maya."

"Scoring first out of India's top 100 IT brains is very impressive."

"Confidentially, Gordon, we would love to have her working full-time, but our Intelligence Agency says she's too valuable to them - but you didn't hear that from me." he winks. Dr. G nods, impressed.

"Maya is a paraplegic since the age of five. It was a terrible motor vehicle accident."

"That's very unfortunate."

"Yes, and she's an only child." says Viraj. "Her parents realized very early she had an astonishing talent with numbers and then with mathematics. She completed eight years of elementary school in only three and then she was accepted at I.I.T. when she was twelve." Viraj smiles. "You and Maya have many similarities, Gordon. I'm sure you will have lots to talk about."

"I'm really looking forward to meeting Maya."

It's eight-thirty-five in the morning and the phone is ringing in Dr. G.'s suite in The Four Seasons Hotel Mumbai, his first full day in India's largest city. Seeing *MAD* on the screen always made him happy. He quickly swipes right and is greeted by the smiling faces of the most important people in his universe.

"Morning, Dad." Madison and Ethan smile in unison. "Siri says it's 8:35 there now, so we figured you've had your breakfast." says Ethan.

"So that makes it, don't tell me, it's hard when there's an extra half-hour and it's thirty-five past the hour here." says dad, grinning. "10:05pm?"

"Correct." says Mad. "So, how was your flight?"

"Very long." shaking his head.

"We did flight tracker. Nine hours just to get to Frankfurt?" grins Ethan.

"And then I had a four hour layover."

"And nine hours to Mumbai." says Madison, stifling a grin.

"I'm so spoiled."

"Shoulda packed your sleeve for the trip home." says Ethan.

"It's weird it's Tuesday there and still Monday here." says Madison. "You've already done Monday, so it's kinda like you're talking to us back in time."

"My body and brain feel out of sorts. Viraj said to drink lots of water and go to bed early this evening … if I can make it to then. Did you speak with mom today?"

"Yeah. She's at a Faculty meeting tonight. She'll

call tomorrow." says Ethan.

"You're coming Sunday morning?"

"Yes." says Madison.

"Great." then he reacts. "Oh, I have to take this call. Love you. Talk soon."

"Bye, Dad." the kids say in unison.

"Morning, Viraj. I'll be right down."

He slaps his face with both hands, then drains the last of his now cold coffee.

Maya's school teacher mother, and electrical engineer father adore their only child. She was fascinated with numbers and symbols even before her first birthday, and prior to her second, her eyes would light up when either of her parents opened their laptop. Maya would come running, little arms outstretched, wanting to sit on their lap and watch the colourful images flash on the screen, as mommy or daddy's fingers danced across the keypad. By her third birthday she was exhibiting signs she had very special talents, and testing soon confirmed it. She was thriving in a school for gifted children when the families' world was shattered in an instant. A motorist driving too fast on a rainy evening failed to stop at an intersection where Maya's family was stopped in their sedan. The SUV plowed into the rear of the sedan, seriously injuring Maya seated in the rear seat. Her spinal cord injury caused paralysis in both legs and has confined her to a motorized wheelchair ever since that terrible evening twelve years ago.

"It's a great honor to meet you, Dr. Giller." says Maya, seated with Dr. G. and Viraj in the boardroom. "Your achievements are very impressive." She wears a pink blouse, black slacks and tan loafers. Her black hair is in a ponytail, and she wears no makeup on her flawless skin. She is clearly a little nervous meeting Dr. Giller.

"Thank you, Maya. I've been very fortunate to work with some very talented people. Viraj tells me you're a rising star."

"I, too, have been very fortunate. It has all happened so quickly for me."

"Winning a big competition is very impressive."

"Thank you, Dr. Giller."

"She almost didn't enter." looking at her.

"My parents encouraged me. I could not believe it when I learned I had won. It has changed my life. Dr. Patel and everyone here have been so kind. I'm very fortunate and very grateful."

"You earned it, Maya." Dr. G. is clearly impressed with Maya's humility.

"Thank you. Have you been to Mumbai before?"

"First time. But I've had many Zooms with Viraj and his team."

"It is such a long flight from America."

"Yes, my son and daughter were tracking it. Nine hours to Frankfurt."

"What are their ages, Dr. Giller?"

"Madison turns eighteen in October … Ethan

will be seventeen next February." his pride evident.

"Are they following in your steps, Dr.?"

"Ethan is. He and his best friend won first prize recently for their Drone Bird invention."

"What kind of Drone Bird?"

"Here, I have a video." taking out his phone he quickly locates the file and plays it for Maya. She watches the short video of the life-like bird with keen interest.

"The bird has a camera in its mouth that can be paired with a computer to provide real-time video. Here he is accepting his award." he proudly plays a short clip.

"That's very impressive."

"The apple didn't fall far from the tree, Gordon." smiles Viraj.

"I'm very proud of him. He's a great son."

"Please tell me about Madison."

"Well, she's what they call the all-American girl. She has her mother's beauty and she's a soccer star."

"Really? I love watching soccer!"

"Maya can recite all the stats for Messi, Ronaldo, Beckham."

"What position does she play?" Maya asks.

"Uh, I'm not sure, but she scores a lot of goals and many of the top colleges have been scouting her for over a year."

"Really?! She must be a Striker."

"Yes, that's it, Striker."

"My favorite players are Strikers. Do you know the most goals scored in international games by a man or woman is actually a woman? Christine Sinclair played many years for Canada and scored 190 goals."

"I'm sure Madison would know her name. Would you like to see a short clip of her last game?"

"Yes of course, please."

He locates the video and plays it for Maya. It's a 15-second clip of Madison scoring a beautiful goal. It ends and he smiles at Maya.

"She is very talented."

"She didn't get it from me." he chuckles.

"Has she made her decision on College?"

"I think it'll be Stanford. She could live with her mother." He looks at Maya. "My wife's an associate Professor at Stanford. We miss her terribly."

"Well, this has been great, Gordon. The team is assembled downstairs. They 're very excited to meet you."

"I'm excited to meet them."

* * *

Fifty engineers and scientists are seated in the auditorium, listening raptly to Dr. G.

"In his first State of The Union address in January, 1961, President Kennedy announced a very ambitious plan to have American astronauts land on the Moon and return home safely.

It seemed impossible. The engineering challenges were immense. Project Apollo would require 500,000 mile flights taking two weeks to complete. It would require technology and systems more powerful, and more accurate, than any that even existed then. And it would require the command ship and the lander to rendezvous and dock twice: once in Earth's orbit, and once in lunar orbit. Think about that for a moment. No such maneuver had even been on a drawing board in 1961. Yet President Kennedy believed that the brightest minds in America would be able to make it happen." He takes out his phone.

"It's hard to believe that the computers NASA deployed in 1969 to program all the complex maneuvers required to land Neil Armstrong and Buzz Aldrin on the Moon, weren't as powerful as the computer that runs our phones."
Maya listens keenly, beside Viraj Patel.

"So when you're faced with a challenge in the coming days and weeks that has you stymied, think of what it must have been like for those scientists and engineers in the 1960's trying to figure out how to do something that had *never* been accomplished before, that seemed impossible." He holds up his phone and smiles. Chuckles and murmurs ripple through the assembled.

"In the same way those brilliant scientists and engineers, and brave astronauts, inspired a new generation of American scientists, engineers and astronauts, know that the great work you are all doing here will inspire Indian boys and girls not yet born to want to become scientists, engineers and astronauts. You're in very good hands with Dr. Patel. I'm grateful for the opportunity to come to Mumbai, and I've really enjoyed being here with all of you today. Thank you very much."

The audience stands and applauds, as Viraj walks over to Dr. G. and shakes hands. Several people come up to Dr. G. to shake hands. Some do selfies. Maya watches, smiling. Dr. G. notices her and motions her over. She glides up to him.

"Your speech was very inspiring, Dr. Giller."

"Thanks, Maya. Viraj and I are having lunch. I'd like you to join us."

"Thank you so much." clearly surprised.

Three floors down, Dr. G. and Maya are enjoying a light lunch with Viraj in his office.

"What do you like to do with your friends in your free time?"

"I don't have any close friends in Mumbai, Dr. Giller. My best friend lives in Satara. It's almost three hours from here. I like to play video games and read mystery novels."

"I enjoy mystery novels, too. I'm a big Michael Crichton fan."

"I am as well. So do Madison and Ethan have a lot of friends?"

"Ethan's best friend, Garret, is his science partner. Madison has lots of friends. Everyone wants to be her friend."

"I'm sure." says Maya, nodding almost wistfully. Dr. G. takes note.

* * *

It's 9:30 Thursday evening in the living room at 16 Fairfield Road. Madison and Ethan are on the sofa doing a Zoom on her laptop with Dad, where it's 8:00am Friday morning in Mumbai, and with mom, where it's 6:30pm. in Palo Alto.

"She's such a nice girl, but her closest friend lives three hours away. In her free time she plays video games and reads mystery novels. When I showed her the video of you getting your award, and you scoring that great goal, her face just lit up."

"That's really nice." says Madison.

"I get the sense she's .. I don't know if it's sadness, or boredom .. but a kid her age needs to be having fun. So I was thinking tomorrow I'd tell her you guys and mom are coming here because we're flying to Thailand for a wedding, and you want to meet her."

"I never like telling a lie, but since we can't tell her about the HT, and she doesn't have any friends, I guess it's justified." says Madison.

"Great, I'll tell her. I'm sure she'll be excited."

* * *

Saturday evening, Mrs. G., Madison and Ethan are relaxing after their 8,814 mile *flight* from Merritt Island to Mumbai, "formerly known as Bombay", Ethan duly notes.

"In case Viraj asks about your flight, I wrote out the details. Memorize it." Madison looks at it.

"Twenty-five hours! That's seven hours longer than yours."

"How much would the tickets have cost, in case they ask?" asks Ethan.

"Eleven hundred economy. Business Class was fifty-seven hundred."

"What?! Why would anyone pay forty-six hundred dollars more for extra foot room, a wider seat and better grub?" Ethan asks.

"That's insane." says his sister. "How much more is that for three tickets?"

"Uh, forty-six hundred times three … thirteen thousand, eight hundred."
Madison shakes her head in grudging awe.

"Okay guys, it's late …" says dad.

"Mad' an' I just had breakfast."

"Yeah, we won't be able to sleep."

"You can't stay up all night, you'll be exhausted by noon." says mom.

"Maya will think it's jet lag." grins Ethan.

"Oh, is it okay to wear these clothes?" asks Madison.

"You could, but with the money I saved on your *flights*, I got all of you new duds. They're in your room." he grins, handing them their room keys.

"Thanks, Dad! says Madison, taking a key and looking at Ethan. "Maybe he got me a sari?" she smiles excitedly as they run to the door, while Mom and Dad watch, enjoying their happiness.

The Mumbai Zoo has been in operation for over 160 years. It was originally located about ten miles away in a Botanical Garden, but when the land was transformed into public housing fifteen years ago, the zoo was relocated. Maya has just arrived in a specially-equipped taxi-van.

"It's so great to meet you, Maya!" says Madison, leaning down to hug her new friend outside the Zoo entrance. "Dad's told us how talented you are."

"Thank you, Madison, it's great to meet you. Your father showed me a video of a wonderful strike you made. You're a fine player."

"Thanks, Maya. This is my brother, Ethan, and my Mom."

"It's great to meet you, Maya." says Ethan.

"So nice to meet you, Maya." says mom.

"The pleasure is all mine! Congratulations on winning the Gold Cup! I want to learn all about your Drone Bird."

"Thanks, sure."

"Your Dad and I have planned a full day. I hope it won't be too tiring after your long flight."

"We should be okay." says Madison, smiling at mom and dad and Ethan.

"Alright, let's get goin'!" says Dr. G.
As they move towards the entrance Ethan looks at a sign. "How much is twenty-five rupees, Maya?"

"It is about point three of an American dollar."

"What? *Thirty cents* for admission!"

"Our Zoo charges thirty-five dollars." Madison looks at Maya.

"Really? That would pay for one hundred visits here."

An hour later Maya, Madison and Ethan are looking at the huge elephants.

"In Indian culture elephants are a symbol of mental strength, earthiness and responsibility." she explains to her new friends, as Ethan reads a large sign.

"Mad', it says they forage up to *nineteen* hours a day, consuming up to 330 pounds of plant matter."

"Wow!"
Dad and Mom are enjoying a cold drink on a bench, watching the teens.

"Look at them. Nine thousand miles from home, making a new friend, and experiencing a new culture." says mom.

"I never really thought about it like this. I just wanted to see if I could actually create it. If I could, it would mean we'd see you more often."

"You've given them an incredible gift, Gordon.

They're going to experience the world like no one else. There's no limitations on where they can go, places they want to see. I'm so proud of you."

The teens are now watching an impressive Cobra slithering on a tree branch in its enclosure.

"Animals occupy a rich tradition in our culture passed down from generations. We grow up reading stories of animals as a divine being in animal form or with animal features. Most are carved in stone, or impressive statues. The cobra is one of the most significant symbols in Hinduism. Snakes are worshipped for their power and protection, and the healing of disease, but they have a dual nature. They are benevolent, and when treated properly they protect the family. But if they are not treated properly they become very dangerous."

"I'm very glad he's behind that glass." says Ethan.

Later the Giller's and Maya are looking at several cows grazing on the grass.

"In our culture, cows represent pure goodness and motherly love. The celestial cow Kamadhenu, is believed to be the mother of all Gods, able to grant any wish to a true seeker."

"Is it true Hindus don't eat animals?" asks Madison.

"Many don't. In Hindu society, vegetarians are regarded to be superior to non-vegetarians. People who eat clean animals like goats and sheep are considered higher compared to those who eat unclean animals like pigs and chickens. They are referred to as carcass eaters, which is considered to be eating impure meat because death makes the animal impure."

"So I guess there's no McDonald's in India?" says Ethan.

"Oh, yes there are. However, most of the food is catered to our traditional choices. But you can get a Chicken Maharaja Mac for 325 Rupees."

"That's a buck US, Mad!" computes Ethan in a nano second.
Madison turns up her nose, and Maya notices.

"They have veggie burgers, too, Madison. In Hindu scriptures a vegetarian diet is based on the concept of *ahimsa*, which means non-violence and compassion towards all beings."

"In America, many people don't eat red meat now." says Mrs. G.

"I stopped five years ago." says Madison.
"What made you decide?"

"I watched a documentary on how cows and chickens are fed to get them ready for slaughter, it was disgusting. Then I ate a veggie burger - it was delicious!"

"She stopped eating meat that day, Maya." says Mrs. G. "Plant-based food is so much healthier."

"Are you vegetarian, Maya?" Madison asks.

"About ninety per cent." she grins. "Ammi has two recipes that have real meat and I just can't give that up!" she laughs.

"I'm getting hungry listening to this. says Dr. G.,
"And Maya's mother has prepared a big feast for us, so we should get going."

* * *

Maya and her parents live in Sanpada, in a three-bedroom bungalow on a nice property with tall trees and thick bushes. On the patio in the backyard, sheltered by an awning from the late afternoon sun, Maya and her parents, Sanjay and Meta Kumar, are enjoying iced tea with the Giller's.

"Meta teaches mathematics at a private school." says Sanjay. "I'm an engineer with an aeronautic company."

"Ethan's very good at math." says Mrs G.

"He can multiply double digits before I get my calculator open." says Madison, as Ethan shrugs and sips his tea.

"Maya says you are an accomplished soccer player, Madison." says Sanjay.

"We have a very good team. We're ranked fifth in our State … Florida."

"Impressive. Maya loves soccer, she knows the statistics of the top players." Meta says.

"What is most impressive, it is a woman who scored the most goals ever in international play." looking at Madison.

"Yes, Christine Sinclair of Canada. She scored 190, in 331 caps."

"Mad's in her third year with the *Rebels* and you've scored, what, 48 now?" looking at his sister.

"Something like that." she shrugs, always so modest. "Did Maya tell you Dad got to know Neil Armstrong?" shifting the focus from herself.

"Yes, that must have been quite a thrill for you, Dr. Giller." says Meta.

"Please, Gordon. Yes, he was my hero growing up. Larger than life in my young eyes." smiling at the memory. "The night before I was to meet him, I was so excited I couldn't sleep. I was a nineteen year old kid. I hoped I could shake his hand. Maybe ask him a question. What struck me was how unassuming he was. He was one of the most famous people in the world, forever a part of history, but you'd never know it by the way he carried himself. After I got to know him over the years, he said he accepted the adulation was part of the job. But it was difficult for him because he was from a very small town in Ohio, the population was under eight thousand." He sips his iced tea, then looks at his kids. "It was an important life lesson for me, and one Laura and I have tried to instil in our children."

"What a wonderful story, Gordon. Thanks for sharing." says Sanjay.

"Maya said your speech inspired everyone." says Meta.

"It was so nice for me to see firsthand the great work Dr. Patel and his team are doing here. NASA gets much of the headlines, of course, so it's easy to overlook the significant contributions scientists and engineers around the world have made towards space exploration. The first man to fly in space was a Russian, Yuri Gagarin. It inspired President Kennedy in 1961 to set the goal of landing a man on the moon by the end of that decade. It was a very tense competition with serious political consequences. Here we are decades later and the United States and much of the world are still not allies of Russia, but our astronauts and Russian astronauts are working and living for weeks on the International Space Station, conducting experiments that will ultimately benefit the world. It's really incredible, and yet it isn't discussed much. So when I meet a seventeen year old girl who is incredibly gifted," he looks at Maya, "I want to share with her my experiences and knowledge because I know it's people like Maya who will be making the next big discoveries."

"Thank you, Dr. Giller." says Maya, as a buzzer blares.

"Supper is ready." smiles Meta, as they stand.

* * *

The large, wooden serving table has six warming pots which the Giller's are investigating, trying to decide on their dinner choices.

"This is Dal Makhani, Madison." says Meta. "Lentils, kidney beans, fresh spinach, and spices. It's all gluten-free."

Madison ladles a serving onto her dinner plate, and hands the ladle to mom. "Smells delicious." she says, as Meta lifts the lid on the next pot.

"This is pan mateer. Tofu cut into cubes and pan fried. With onions and peas in a rich sauce."

"Madison loves tofu, Meta." says Mom, as Madison ladles some.

"The next two pots are meat recipes, Ethan." says Maya.

"My fave." he grins, as Meta lifts the lid on the first. "Aloo tikki is one of the most popular street foods in India. It's made with boiled potatoes - aloo means potato - then they're mashed and mixed with peas, then formed into small patties and fried in a vanaspati bath." says Meta.

"Yanaspati?" asks Ethan with a furrowed brow.

"It's a Sanskrit word that refers to all vegetation, but Vanaspati only refers to plants that bear fruit, not light flowers." says Meta. Ethan ladles two of the patties onto his plate.

"This is Chicken Biryani." says Meta, lifting the lid on the next pot. "It's one of the most popular Indian dishes. Very tender chicken with basmati rice in a rich, spicy sauce."

"Is this one of the two recipes you can't live without, Maya?" grins Ethan.

"Yes, it is!" laughs Maya.

"Oh, she could *never* give this up!" laughs Meta, as Ethan serves a portion onto his plate.

How They Came To Be

* * *

Later the seven diners are well into their meal.

"This is so delicious Mrs. Kumar." says Madison.

"Are these recipes passed along by your grandparents?" Mrs. G asks

"Yes, some of them are. If you'd like I could e-mail them to you, Laura."

"Yes, please." as Ethan grins beside her. "Now I can say I'm a meat and aloo guy." and everyone chuckles.

"You have a nice energy, Ethan." says Sanjay. Before Ethan can reply, three pings chime from Maya's phone. Suddenly, the carefree vibe the Kumar family is enjoying vanishes as Maya looks at her parents. The Giller's take note, too, as Maya looks apologetically at her guests.

"I'm very sorry, you'll have to excuse me. I have to make a phone call."

"Of course." says Dr. G., as Maya quickly reverses her wheelchair. "Please don't leave without saying goodbye." She quickly glides down the hallway, leaving the diners looking a little perplexed.

"In addition to her work with the Space Agency," says Sanjay, "Maya also works with another government Agency."

"Very remarkable young lady." nods Dr. G.

"There's lots more food, everyone. I'll keep Maya's dinner warm." Meta says, standing to gather Maya's dinner plate. "We never know how long she'll be when they call."

Maya glides into her bedroom and closes the door. The room is spacious, with a small bed, two night tables and a dresser. As she motors forward, her right hand presses a button on the underside of the left arm of her wheelchair. Suddenly, the wall behind her dresser begins to silently slide open, revealing a ten foot wide office with a work station with two computers, two large monitors and several clocks on the wall displaying Time Zones for each country. She uses the same button to close the sliding door behind her as she positions herself at the work station and quickly puts on a headset. She rapidly types on a keyboard and in seconds she's on a Zoom call with a man, 40's, in a dark suit, and a woman, early 30's, in a dark blouse, seated at a table.

"Hello, Maya. I hope we haven't taken you from a Sunday supper with your mother and father?" says Arash Khan, a fifteen year veteran of the Intelligence Agency.

"Just finished, sir."

"Good. Please check your inbox." Maya quickly opens her e-mail.

"We managed to retrieve this communique minutes ago from a server linked to a man we know has had dealings with Sharma."
The communique opens on the monitor to Maya's left. It's only two lines of unreadable computer code

that would be gibberish to only a few as brilliant as Maya. As her fingers dance over the keyboard, the first line has been transformed to Sanskrit, which Maya reads aloud when her keystrokes stop.

"Cargo being transported Karnala .. thirteenth .. twenty-two hundred hours. Forty-seven packages .. thirty-nine packages. That's all sir."

"Excellent, Maya." says Khan, pleased. "So they transported 86 children to Karnala last evening."

"But we don't know the departure location, and if they *left* at twenty-two hundred, or were to *arrive* at Karnala at twenty-two hundred." says Janice Courtnall, a British expat.

"I'll hack into CCTV for all routes leading into Karnala from twenty-one hundred last night. See if there's one or two transports large enough to hold that many children." tapping keystrokes which has activated motion on the monitor on her right. "Okay, shouldn't take me long, sir."

"Thanks." says Khan, as Maya exits the Zoom and continues to type quickly. Then video pops onto the monitor of vehicles moving on a freeway in darkness, the only light provided by the vehicles and light poles every 150 feet or so. The video fast forwards, whizzing past countless sedans and SUV's, but no trucks fit the description.

Thirty minutes later the six diners have moved to the small living room.

"Have you been to Thailand before, Ethan?" asks

Sanjay.

"No. I'm really looking forward to it." as Maya joins them. "Sorry about that." looking subdued.

"Everything okay, Maya?" her father asks. Maya slightly shrugs and nods. It's clearly not alright, and weighing on her.

"I have your supper warming." smiles Meta.

"I am not hungry now, Ammi, thank you. Would you like to sit outside?" looking at Madison and Ethan.

"Sure." says Madison. She and Ethan follow Maya out of the room. The parents watch them silently until they hear the back door open and close.

"I don't know how she does it." says Meta to her guests.

"She's not permitted to provide us any details of her work, so we don't know the burdens that she takes on." says Sanjay.

"All we know is it's of extreme importance to our government." adds Meta.

"Sometimes we wish we hadn't convinced her to enter the competition. Her life would be so normal." says Sanjay.

"I can only speak to her work with the Agency." says Dr. G. "Dr. Patel is very impressed with her work. I can understand you want Maya to have a normal childhood, because those years are very special. But, like me, she has a God-given gift, so I speak from experience. I was seventeen when I graduated from M.I.T. and NASA offered me a wonderful opportunity."

"You were only seventeen?" asks Meta, clearly shocked.

"Yes. When I was seven I was enrolled in a private school for what they called gifted kids. Five years later I was a Freshman at M.I.T., living off campus with my mom's sister and her husband."

"I can't imagine." marvels Meta.

"Every Monday morning I'd hear my classmates talk about getting drunk at a weekend party." he chuckles. "I was going to Disney movies with my aunt and uncle." Sanjay and Meta chuckle. "Did you make any friends?" asks Meta.

"It was difficult for me because I didn't play sports and I was studying very hard to prepare for my exams. My parents called me twice a week - I was very homesick."

"So you never got to live the life of a little boy?" says Meta.

"No. When NASA offered me a job I was so excited because it was my dream to work with them. Maybe I'd get to meet my hero. But my parents had serious concerns."

"Of course. How could you be emotionally prepared to work with people so many years older than you?" says Sanjay.

"It was very intimidating for me at first. I'd be in meetings with people who were twenty and thirty years older, and they're looking at me like *shouldn't you be in the mail room, kid?* But after a few months I was able to establish myself and get the respect I needed, and fortunately it all worked out for me. And I know it will for Maya."

"I can't thank you enough for sharing that, Gordon." says Meta.

"My pleasure. I've given Maya my coordinates and told her if she ever needs to talk, if she's feeling overwhelmed, she can e-mail or call me." Meta inhales and lets out a sigh, releasing a lot of tension she's been shouldering.

"Thank you so much, Gordon." says Sanjay. Mrs. G. stifles a yawn, and Dr. G. takes note. "We've got an early flight. I think we should hit the road, Mrs. Giller."

In the Kumar's backyard, Maya is laughing with Madison and Ethan. "Today has been the best day for me in over one year."

"'E' and I really enjoyed it, too, Maya."

"Yeah, it's been great."

"I hope we can stay in touch. I can give you my e-mail and cell."

"Great. I'll give you mine." says Madison. "Are you on social?"

"No, my work does not permit me." she shrugs.

"Oh, okay."

"I wish you weren't so far away. I'm thinking I will never see you again."

Madison looks briefly at Ethan, then smiles at Maya..

"Mom and dad have a gazillion Air Miles, so …"

That brings a smile to Maya, as the parents walk out.

"We have to get back to the hotel, guys." says Mom. Madison and Ethan go to Maya. Madison leans down for a long, tight hug.

"I'll e-mail you in a few days. Then we can plan our next visit."

"I can't wait." as Ethan leans down for a nice embrace with her. "Great to meet you, Maya." Then he whispers. "Don't worry, you'll be seeing Mad' an' me again." he winks, and Maya beams a big smile.

* * *

The next morning, Madison and Ethan are in Mom and Dad's hotel room enjoying room service breakfast.

"Right now it's ten o'clock Sunday evening back home." says Ethan. "So tomorrow morning we'll be having a second breakfast on Monday."

"I'm so glad you guys brought my sleeve."

"So after porting 38 times, did it feel weird being in a plane?" asks Madison.

"Yeah, a little. But I think the hardest think with porting is no credit cards."

"Definitely." says mom. "It's a cash-less world."

"When you two eventually port on your own always have at least two hundred cash each to pay for food, taxis and trains." dad says.

"When will we be able to port solo?" Madison

asks.

"I want you to take a few more flights so you're comfortable."

The room phone rings. Dr. G. gets up and answers.

"Hello?" he listens, then, "That's very thoughtful, Viraj, you didn't have to." He listens. "Okay, see you then." He hangs up and looks at his family uneasily.

"He's driving us to the airport, and looking forward to meeting you guys."

"We don't have any luggage!" says Mrs. G., looking very concerned.

* * *

"Is this your first time going to Thailand?" smiles Viraj at Madison and Ethan as they walk out of the Four Seasons Mumbai Hotel with their parents. The kids nod, smiling. "You'll love it!" as they reach the Taxi-Van. The driver takes Dr. G.'s suitcase and stows it. Viraj realizes there's no more luggage.

"Where's your luggage?" looking at Mrs. G. and the kids.

"We checked it at the airport." mom smiles.

"No point lugging it in for a day." says Dr. G.

"We just took out the clothes we'd need." adds mom, over-selling the *little white lie*. They pile into the van and it drives off.

Thirty minutes later Giller's are outside the Departures at Maharaja International Airport, waving good-bye to Viraj. He gets in the Van and it drives off, and the Giller's begin to walk towards the Terminal entrance.

"How much will you get cashing in your ticket, Dad?" asks Ethan.

"Not sure. I'm giving it to you guys to put away until you HT alone."

"Really?" Madison smiles.

"Thanks, Dad." says Ethan.

"Hey, thank you for convincing me to port home." he grins as they walk inside.

* * *

The following afternoon, Rebecca and Natalie are in the locker room when Madison walks in.

"Mad', you didn't call me back. Where were you yesterday?" asks Rebecca.

"Dad says E' and I spend too much time on our phones, so he's got us turning them off for twenty-four hours on Sunday now."

"Really?" says Natalie.

No, but if I told you we were in India for thirty-six hours and how we got there my Dad would ground me, so I'm gonna keep telling little white lies.

"Actually, it's not that bad. Our parents didn't have phones when they were our age, and they found things to do, right?" says Madison.

"If my dad did that I'd buy a trap phone so fast!" says Rebecca.

An hour into the *Rebels* scrimmage, Rebecca makes a clever chip pass to Madison for a clear strike twenty feet from the keeper. But Madison's effort sends the ball wide. She's visibly frustrated.

Later, practice is over and Coach Jamieson walks with Madison.

"You looked a little sluggish, Mad'. Didn't pound nine last night?"

Actually Coach, I didn't sleep a wink on Saturday night … and I had two breakfasts yesterday, nine thousand miles apart … and I just.. want.. to.. sleep.

"Yeah, I'll be fine tomorrow, Coach."

"I'm counting on it."

* * *

7. MAYA'S BURDEN

4,371 miles from Merritt Island, it's almost midnight as Maya looks at a 'still' image from CCTV footage. She's on a Zoom with Khan and Courtnall.

"RTO says the number plate is registered to a delivery company that reported one of their trucks stolen yesterday." says Khan.

"If you can e-mail me the location where the truck was reported stolen, in the morning before I leave for work I'll check CCTV and see if I can grab the number plate of the thief's vehicle, or a visual of him." stifling a yawn.

"Sorry we had to wake you." says Khan.

"I wish to catch these despicable people as much as you, sir."

"Sleep well, Maya. We'll talk in the morning." says Courtnall.

"You as well. 'Night." Maya exits the Zoom. She turns out the light, then reverses her wheelchair and turns around. She glides out of her secret space and with a press of the button on her wheelchair arm, the wall almost silently slides closed in seven seconds. There's a soft two-tap knock on her bedroom door.

"Come in Ammi." The door opens and Meta

enters, wearing a robe and a worried look.

"Is there anything I can do, dear?"

"Yes, give me a nice smile. I don't want you worrying about me."

"It's not right they call you so late."

"If I could tell you why they call, you would understand."

"Now I will worry even more." sighs Meta.

"Ammi, my life will never be in danger. Nor you and papa. Find peace in knowing I am using the gifts I was blessed with to help those who are in need of our assistance."

Meta looks at her daughter and gives her the smile she asked for. Maya smiles, extends her arms, and mother and daughter embrace warmly.

"I'm doing a Zoom tomorrow with Madison and Ethan." Maya smiles, which brings an authentic smile from Ammi.

* * *

It's eight-thirty in the morning in Merritt Island and Madison and Ethan are on a Zoom with Maya, where it's seven o'clock that evening in Mumbai.

"How was the wedding?" smiles Maya.

"It was good." Madison says, not happy she has to tell a lie to a friend. She quickly changes the subject so she doesn't have to compound the lie *with a detailed description of a wedding that never actually happened.*

"How have you been? Still working long hours?"

"Yes, but we had a small victory today." Maya smiles.

"Can never have too many of those." says Madison. "Anything you can share?"

"No, sorry."

"We understand. There's lots of stuff dad has to keep from us until it's announced." with a subtle glance at her brother.

"I'm sure. So, when is the *Rebels* next match?"

"Friday, versus Lakefield. They're on our heels in second place."

"Good luck. And how have you been, Ethan?"

"Good, just gettin' the circadian reset to local time."

"I've never flown, but I'm told passing through many Time Zones it takes several days to feel normal."

"Dad's an expert on it. NASA tracks the astronauts' sleep patterns during missions, and they've found they sleep about one hour less." Madison says.

"That's interesting. When I first heard about circadian rhythm I thought it was to do with the cicada bug that rubs it's wings rapidly to make that annoying sound." Maya grins.

"Circadian comes from the Latin *circa,* meaning around, and *dies* meaning days." says Ethan.

"And it's not just humans - animals and plants are regulated by circadian rhythm as well." says Madison.

"You have taught me something very useful today, thanks."

"We have to get to class, Maya. Great seeing you." Madison says.

"Great to see you guys. And Ethan, you will be taking video of Madison's match for me?"

"For sure." and the Zoom ends.

* * *

It's a sunny morning in Majorca, and Rafael is in month five in his nine month Training to become a Police Officer. Fifty Trainees have assembled on a soccer pitch to learn the proper manoeuvres to overpower a criminal without using a firearm. Each man wears black shorts and a white Tee with a large, black number on the back. Rafael's number is '7'. The Trainees are closely watching as a veteran Officer demonstrates on a Trainee playing the role of *criminal*. A flurry of very precise leg and arm movements has the Trainee on his back in seconds. It's very impressive. The Trainees are instructed to pair up, and each 'criminal' is given a rubber knife. Rafael nods to the guy beside him, who has been given a rubber knife. He's mid-20's, taller than Rafael, and packing a few more pounds around his waist.

"Knife holders be aggressive. Officers attempt to subdue without incident." A whistle blares and the 25 partners square off under the close gaze of a dozen Staff moving about. Rafael moves smoothly in short steps, eyes riveted on the 'knife', not blinking. His opponent brandishes the knife menacingly, playing the role very well. Suddenly he sees his opening as Rafael moves to his (Rafael) right and the guy thrusts the knife towards Rafael's right side. But Rafael is too quick for him. In a flash, he's moved cat-like to his left and grabbed the guy's right arm, twisting it back and he executes a slick leg kick that buckles his opponent's legs and he falls to the ground, as Rafael takes control of the knife. Two Staff are very impressed and make a note on their clipboards. Rafael graciously offers a hand up to his partner who is clearly impressed with Rafael. Now Rafael has the knife, and his partner is looking to even the score. Rafael sneers menacingly at the 'Officer', goading him to attack. Rafael makes a sudden thrust with the knife and the 'Officer' deploys both arms to try to gain control of the knife. But he's a second to slow, as Rafael moves in a flash and the 'Officer' is pinned with the knife held at his throat. Rafael gives him another hands-up as a Staff makes an entry about number '7' on his clipboard.

The dry land training is over and the 50 guys are filing off the field. One of the two Staff who observed Rafael's superb effort approaches him.

"Where'd you learn those moves, Garcia?"

"My papa started me very young, sir. He told me a man must be able to defend himself without the use of a weapon."

"Good advice." he smiles and walks off.

"Thank you, sir." pleased.

* * *

Ethan is standing on the sidelines taking phone video of the big scoreboard, which shows the score is tied 3-3 between Lakefield and the visiting *Rebels*.

"Tie score, just under four minutes to play. It's what we call a nail-biter, Maya." adding a little audio to his Sports Center production.

Coach Jamieson is exhorting her sweaty charges as they take on fluids during a timeout on the warm afternoon.

"4-Flood, just like we practiced." as the Referee's whistle pierces the air. The *Rebels* jog onto the field. Rebecca gets into position for her corner kick. Players move left, quickly cut right, jockeying for position. Madison is double-teamed. Rebecca kicks the ball in a high, arcing trajectory. Madison pivots quickly to elude a defender, then springs up and adroitly heads the ball fifteen feet to her right to a teammate who's all alone and she kicks the ball into the gaping net.

Ethan continues to film as the *Rebels* celebrate.

"They were so sure the corner kick was set up for Madison to take a shot they double-teamed her, which left her teammate wide open." grins Ethan.

Now he films himself. "I'll text you the clips and you can watch them at breakfast, Maya." he grins.

* * *

It's Saturday morning in Mumbai and Maya is watching Ethan's video on her laptop, seated with her parents at the dining table where they had dinner with the Giller's two weeks ago. Ethan's audio fills the room. "They were so sure the corner kick was set up for Madison to take a shot they double-teamed her, which left her teammate wide open." The video ends and Maya grins at her parents.

"Would you like for me to play it again?"

"How many times have you replayed it?" Meta grins.

"I have no idea. At least 12, maybe more." she laughs.

Her parents are clearly pleased to see Maya so happy. "Yes, let's see it once more." grins papa.

"Okay, and then we will call them."

* * *

Madison is on the sofa in the living room, between her brother and dad, on a Zoom with Maya and her parents.

"She's played it at least twenty times!" grins Meta.

"She hasn't stopped smiling since the first time." says Sanjay. "Her cheeks will be sore tomorrow."

"I'm happy you liked it, Maya." Madison says.

"You did a perfect header, Madison!"

"It was very good strategy by our Coach." says Madison modestly.

"Yes, it was a very good call. Oh, and I must not forget your commentary, Ethan, it was excellent. You could have a career as a sports commentator."

"Thanks, but I think I'll stick with science."

"How have you been, Meta and Sanjay?" asks Dr. G. "Very well, thank you." says Meta. "How is Laura?"

"She's well, and keeping very busy." says Dr. G.

"You must miss her terribly?" says Sanjay.

"Very much. But she gets home once a month."

"She has a gazillion Air Miles." says Madison.

"Yes, she racks them up, for sure." says Dr. G., looking at his kids.

"Gordon, in two weeks it is Maya's 18th birthday, and she would like so much for Madison and Ethan to come. Meta and I will pay for their flights."

"Oh, that would be wonderful." looking at his kids smiling.

"Really?!" says Meta, relief and joy washing over her face.

"Thank you so much, Maya, we'd love to come." says Madison.

"But we will pay for the flights, Sanjay, I insist." says Dr. G.

"You are so kind, Gordon." says Meta.

"I'm so happy, I'm going to cry." says Maya.

"I am, too." says Meta. "Thank you so much,

Gordon."

"Of course. We only have one 18th birthday, right?" he grins.

"It will be a small party with lots of great food." says Meta. "And please, no gifts, your presence is the best gift."

"Okay, but if you wanna go to the Zoo again, I'll spring for the admissions." says Ethan. The Kumar's laugh. "I really like your sense of humor, Ethan." says Maya, grinning.

* * *

Moments later, Madison, Ethan and Dad are in the kitchen. "Thanks for letting us go, Dad." Madison says.

"Of course! When I saw how happy she was, and Meta and Sanjay, how could I say no? The HT is turning out to be so much more than I ever imagined."

"What do you mean?"

"I don't know what Maya's work with the Intelligence Department entails, nor do her parents. But I sense the pressure she's experiencing is far greater than what I had at NASA as a seventeen year old kid. But she can't talk about it. And she has no close friends to hang out with like a normal teen. I know what that's like, so I knew I had to help her. I knew she'd love you guys, because everyone loves you. And look what's happened because you said yes to coming to Mumbai? You've made a new friend and brightened Maya's life.

"You deserve way more credit than us because you didn't have to do it." says Madison.

"Totally, cuz I really didn't care if we went, but I'm glad we did." says Ethan.

"It may not develop into a long-term friendship, but our family can say, for a brief moment in time, we helped bring joy to a young girl and her parents, and that's a beautiful thing." Madison hugs him.

"You're the best Dad ever." Dad reaches out his left arm and Ethan joins the hug.

"We should go online and find out how many Air Miles it would cost to fly to Mumbai, in case Maya asks us." says Madison.

"Good thinking." dad says, ending the hug.

"Likely a million … and five million for Business Class." says Ethan, as dad walks off.

"We're so lucky Maya and Rafael don't use social, E'."

"Yeah, if Rafael was posting his pic on IG and messaging you, 'Bec and Nat' would be all over you wanting to meet him."
Dad watches them, smiling. "When will you be speaking with Rafael next?"

"In a couple of hours." Madison says.

"Say hi for mom and me."

"For sure."

* * *

Ethan's video is playing on a laptop. "They were so sure the corner kick was set up for Madison to take a shot they double-teamed her, which left her teammate wide open."

Rafael is sitting at his kitchen table, grinning, clapping his hands.

"That was a great play, Madison!" He closes his laptop and picks up his phone. Madison and Ethan fill the screen.

"Thanks, but we can't wait to hear your news?"

"Yeah, how's the training goin'?" says Ethan.

"Very well, thanks. They've cut twenty-one guys, so there's twenty-nine left."

"They're hiring twelve, right?" asks Madison.

"Yes."

"So what's combat training like?" Ethan asks.

"They put us in situations we could face, like disarming a guy with a knife on the street or in their home."

"Sounds scary." says Madison.

"The knives are rubber, but, yeah, it's pretty intense."

"Your Judo training must help a lot?" Ethan asks.

"Yes, papa started training me when I was seven."

"You won that competition, so you must be very good." says Madison.

"I'm currently eighth dan black."

"What does that mean?" asks Ethan.

"It means I can handle most guys." he grins.

"You handled the guy on the street pretty fast."

says Madison.

"That was, how do you say .. a piece of candy?"

"A piece of cake." grins Madison.

"Close. So what's new with you guys? Any trips planned?"

"Uh, no, just the usual, you know?" says Madison. "The playoffs start in a few days."

"Good luck with the games. Could you do another video for me, Ethan?"

"Sure."

"Thanks. I'll look forward to watching it. Okay, I have an early morning, guys. I have to get to bed."

"Have a great week, Rafael." Madison waves.

* * *

Two days later the *Rebels* are on their Home Field playing their first playoff game against Jupiter High. Ethan is on the sidelines filming himself on his phone.

"Jupiter finished fourth in the season's standings, eight games behind the Conference leading *Rebels,* so they are definitely the underdog in this match."

Mrs. G. ported home for the match and is sitting with Dr. G. "Go, Mad'!" then she looks at him. "We need to get the first goal."

"I think you're more nervous than Mad'."

"I'm more nervous than when I played."

"Don't worry, Mad' had her game face on at

breakfast."

"Match face, dear."

They've played just over five minutes and there's no score, but the *Rebels* are on a fast break down field. Madison's running hard, caressing the ball with her feet as she looks for an opening. She spots Rebecca running past a slow defender. In a flash, Madison kicks the ball with her right foot, leading Rebecca beautifully to an open area. With a burst of speed, Madison dashes past another defender.

"Bec!" Mad shouts. Rebecca stops on a dime and the defender is caught out of position, allowing Rebecca an opening. She slides a twenty foot pass to Madison who takes it without breaking stride. She fakes to her right and then pivots back to her left and in one motion drills a low hooking shot that sails past the diving keeper to give the *Rebels* that first goal mom wanted. Her teammates rush to mob Madison, only seventy-five feet from where Ethan is filming the action, as only he can.

"And she put it past the helpless keeper to give the *Rebels* the lead."

Up in the stands, Mom and Dad are very excited.

"What a great play! Incredible strike!" beams mom.

Later, Ethan is on the sidelines doing another video report for his faraway friends.

"With only two minutes left, the *Rebels* are

cruising to victory, leading 3-0 in the sudden death match. Madison scored the first two goals in the game's opening twelve minutes to demoralize Jupiter."

Mom and Dad are with Ethan after the game, as Madison walks up with her two BFF's.

"Hey, Mrs. G., nice to see you." says Rebecca.

"Hey, Mrs. G., ditto." says Natalie.

"Great to see you guys. Lovely pass for Mad's first."

"Thanks." says Rebecca.

"Get some good vid for your uncle, E'?" asks Natalie. Ethan's caught off guard, but recovers nicely. "Oh, yeah." he grins.

"Okay, Mad', later." says Rebecca, as her BFF's walk away.

"A little heads-up woulda been nice, Mad'."

"Nat' just asked me in the locker room why you were filming. I had to think of something."

"It's just a little white lie." grins dad as they walk away.

The next morning the Giller's are on the back deck, Zooming with Maya.

"Ammi said to tell you she's going to have a new menu experiences for you." her smiling face filling Madison's MacBook screen.

"What, no aloo tikki?" gasps Ethan in mock despair. "I gotta have my aloo!"

Maya laughs. "Alright, I will tell her, Ethan."

"We're counting down the days, Maya." grins Madison.

"Me, too. And promise me, no gifts."

"We promise." says Ethan.

"Okay, I have to go now. Thank you again for the video, Ethan. Great match, Madison."

"Bye, Maya." the Giller's say together. The screen goes dark.

"If you could have seen how she looked when I met her, you'd know how much meeting you guys has meant to her. It's extraordinary."

"She's a really good person, Dad." says Madison.

"She is." says Ethan.

"As long as her parents don't post anything on social." says mom.

"Meta and Sanjay have never done social media, Laura." Madison's phone rings. She picks it up.

"It's Rafael." smiling, she answers. "Hi, Rafael, how are you?"

"You're all outside! Hi Mr. and Mrs. Giller, Ethan! How is everyone?"

"Great!" says Ethan, as mom and dad give a little wave, smiling.

"Is this not a good time?"

"No, we just finished lunch." says Madison.

"I just watched Ethan's video of your match. You played amazing!"

"Thanks, Rafael. So, how's training going? Have they dismissed more candidates?"

"Yes. There's only twenty left."

"How does it look, Rafael?" asks dad.

"Pretty good, I'm in the top five in hand-to-hand combat."

"That's great!" says Madison.

"And I scored ninety-two on my written exam.

But I need to improve my shooting skills. I'd never fired a gun before I started my training last year."

"Really?" says Madison.

"Papa never liked guns. It's why he trained me in Judo. But I know I can improve my scores, I'm not too concerned."

"We pray for you every night." says Madison.

"That's very kind of you. I'll be praying you have a safe trip to Mumbai. When do you leave?"

"Friday morning, which is Saturday morning there." says Madison.

"How long is the flight?"

"I don't even wanna think about it!" she laughs.

"What happened to the guy who stole Mad's bag, Rafael?" asks dad.

"He will be sentenced in two weeks."

"Hope he turns his life around." says mom.

"Yes." says Rafael. "Okay, looks like you have a very nice day there. I won't keep you." he smiles and gives a little wave.

"Thanks, Rafael. Have a great week." says Madison. "We'll call you next week."

"Good luck, man!" says Ethan.

"Thanks, safe travels." the screen goes dark. Madison looks at her Dad. "I think we'll have to start calling the HT *LWL.*"

"*LWL?*"his brow furrowed.

"Little white lies." shaking her head.

"We don't have a choice." says dad, standing.

"Enjoy your day. I have to get started on my research for your trip."

"What research?" Ethan asks.

"Places we're going to visit?" says Madison.

"No, I have to locate a safe place for you guys to port to that isn't too far from stores where you can buy two suitcases, some clothes and toiletries. Then I need to calculate how far Maya's home is from that store so I know how much cash you'll need, because you can't Uber, right? And I want to source a location that's much closer to the airport for you to port home."

"You've really thought this through, Dad." says Ethan, very impressed.

"You're in a foreign country with no cell phones or credit cards. There's no room for error."

"Thanks, Dad." says Madison.

8.   FIRST SOLO PORTING

It's eight o'clock Friday morning and Madison and Ethan are with dad in the living room doing final prep for their first solo HT flight.

"It's six-thirty this evening in Mumbai. I told Sanjay not to come to the airport because connecting flights could be delayed. I found two stores in a strip mall a few miles from Maya's home that sell luggage and clothing."

"Where are we porting to?" Ethan asks.

"I've given you GC's (Global Coordinates) to a soccer pitch a half-mile from the mall. You'll need fifty-five bucks to buy two suitcases." He peels off some cash and hands to Madison. "Here's a hundred to buy a change of clothes. I checked the taxi rates from the strip mall to Maya's home … this will cover the fare." He peels off more cash.

"Here's five hundred for emergencies." gives her cash. "Sanjay will insist on driving you to the airport. Let him - you know how to handle it. Here's your D.A.C.'s. Don't put it in until after you arrive at the pitch, and call me immediately."

"9-1-1-D-A-D." Madison says.

"Correct."

"Here's your BNP (Body Neutralizing Pill) for your

return port." hands them a small plastic bottle with two pills.

Five minutes later Madison and Ethan are on the deck. Dr. G. watches them forcefully exhale all the air in their lungs. Then they quickly tap the 'Launch' key, and a second later … they've vanished! He looks to the skies, many thoughts.

* * *

It's a very hot evening in a Mumbai suburb as three young girls in shorts and t-shirts run after a bouncing soccer ball on a spotty pitch that doesn't require weekly mowing. Three dozen or so adults are loudly cheering on the twenty-two youngsters on the pitch, all eyes focused on the frenzied action. Which is fortunate, because a few seconds ago the number of spectators increased by two, with the arrival of Madison and Ethan after their ten second *flight* from America! They're at the far end of the pitch, where their arrival has gone unnoticed.

"Lucky dad's GC's weren't at that end." says Madison, putting in her DAC. "It's a good omen." says Ethan.

Madison has opened her cast-sleeve, and the keypad is ready for her to call. "9-1-1-D-A-D." she says, tapping the keys. "This is so cool!" she grins. Ten seconds later dad's technology has re-routed her call to his DAC. "Hey, dad, we're here."

"G.C.'s worked out okay?"

115

"Perfect, wouldn't expect anything less."

"Call when you get to Maya's."

"We will." The call ends and she looks at Ethan.

"Let's get the luggage."

Fifteen minutes later Madison and Ethan are inside the luggage store.

"Dad said the suitcases he saw online were fifty-five bucks total." says Ethan. "Say twenty-eight bucks each, we're looking for one that's, uh …" he's doing the mental calculation, "around twenty-four hundred rupees."

"That's sick how you can do it so fast!" grins Madison, as he looks at prices.

"That must be it." pointing at a pink, pulley-suitcase under a sign; ₹ 2,355.00.

"I'll get that one." says Madison. "What color do you want?"

"Anything but pink."

* * *

"You're here!" exults Maya, smiling broadly, as Madison and Ethan walk into the foyer with big smiles, pulling their pink and yellow suitcases. Madison rushes to Maya and they embrace warmly, while Ethan shakes hands with Sanjay and hugs Meta. "How was your flight?" Meta asks him.

"Successful." Maya and her parents chuckle.

"You look surprisingly fresh." says Sanjay.

"We slept and drank lots of water." says Madison,

116

then quickly, "So, how's the birthday girl?" wanting to get the convo away *from their flight.*

"Even better now that you're here."

"I'll put your luggage in your rooms." offers Sanjay.

"That's okay, Mr. Kumar." says Madison quickly. "We need to freshen up, don't we, E?" He nods.

"I'll show you to your rooms." says Meta.

* * *

In the living room at 16 Fairfield Road, Dad is on the sofa, nervously tapping his right hand on his thigh, waiting for the call confirming his kids are safe and sound in the Kumar's home over 8,800 miles away. Suddenly he sits up, as his daughter's voice crackles in his right ear via his DAC.

"Hey, dad, we're at the Kumar's."

"Great." trying to sound as if she's just checking in from a friend's home two streets away.

"Everything go smoothly?"

"GC's were perfect and we got the luggage, so you can stop worrying."

"Wasn't worried at all." he grins.

"Yeah, right. I'll let you go so you can call mom."

"Okay, have fun, and call before you leave to come home."

"We will. Tell mom we miss her."

"Of course." He takes out his DAC and exhales.

* * *

Next morning Madison is seated beside Maya, opposite Ethan and Sanjay at the Kumar's dining table, which is loaded with serving dishes with lids. Meta lifts the lid on the first dish.

"This is low calorie Oats Idli with grated carrots." she says, as Madison and Ethan lean in to inhale the hot, fresh aroma.

"Hmm, smells delicious." says Madison, as Ethan nods in agreement. Meta scoops a serving into Madison's bowl.

"Maya has idli every morning. It's very rich in vitamins and minerals." says Meta, as she lifts the lid on another serving dish.

"This is Methi Ka Thepla, a soft flatbread made with ginger, chilies, herbs and yogurt. Would you both like to try it?"

"Yes, let me serve it for you." says Ethan, picking up the silver tongs. Meta lifts the lid on the third serving dish.

"Sali Par Edu, grated, deep fried potatoes topped with eggs, sunny side up."

"This is amazing!" says Madison.

"Did you not go to bed last night, Mrs. Kumar?" grins Ethan. They laugh. "Ammi loves to cook, Ethan." says Maya.

"If I lived here I'd weigh two hundred pounds." he says, taking a bite. They all laugh as they dig in to the sumptuous breakfast.

The Sharmand Medical and Rehabilitation Center in downtown Mumbai has been a second home for Maya since she lost the use of her legs almost thirteen years ago. Tuesday, Thursday and Saturday she receives therapy focused on improving her lower body mobility through repetitive, task specific exercises. Madison and Ethan are sitting with Meta, watching.

"Maya has incomplete paraplegia, which means she has some feelings from the waist down" says Meta. "Over the years there's been tremendous advances in treatment, like this walking therapy, which she does every Saturday."
Maya is secured to a harness-pulley affixed to a sturdy beam above. She's 'walking' on a slowly moving treadmill as kneeling therapists on each side grasp her legs in both hands and create the walking movement for her, while a third therapist stands behind, supporting her.

"This therapy helps her relearn the motion of walking." says Meta. "The belief is it will re-train her body to walk on its own without cognitive thought."

"How long has she been doing the walking therapy?" Madison asks.

"Two years. On Tuesday and Thursday she does stretching exercises and lifts weights to maintain her upper body strength and tone." They're watching

Maya, who has a very determined look as she 'walks' on the treadmill.

On the way home they stop for ice cream, a post-workout ritual for Maya and her mama.

"When they lower the pulley, do you feel the weight of your body on your legs at all?" Madison asks.

"No. But the hope is through repetition the nerve endings may re-grow. Did Ammi tell you I'm also doing electrical stimulation and stem cell therapy?"

"Yes, it sounds very promising." Madison smiles.

"When you see what's happened with artificial intelligence," says Ethan, "I think the next ten years will be amazing."

"We pray for that every day." says Meta softly, patting Maya's hand.

"We'll be there when you take your first steps unaided." Madison says.

"Thanks, Madison." smiles Maya. "I will add that to my prayers."

Maya's boss, Viraj Patel, is one of nine people gathered in the Kumar's darkened dining room for the cake cutting part of Maya's birthday party. Maya has loaned Madison an orange jacket, and Ethan wears Sanjay's white Bandhgala jacket with bright red images of flowers and plants. Maya is seated at the head of the table where a round, silver plate sits. Meta is leading Pujas (prayers) and an Aarti (a prayerful ceremony of light) is being performed. The

Aarti is a small flame burning on a wick which Sanjay places on the plate and rotates it around Maya. Then Sanjay takes a tiny amount of tika, made of rice mixed with yogurt and coloured powder, and places it on Maya's forehead. Ethan looks discreetly at Madison, both intrigued by this Indian custom.

Moments later, they're serenading a grinning Maya with a rousing rendition of a song that's universally known;

"Happy birthday to you, happy birthday to you, happy birthday dear Maya, happy birthday to you." Everyone cheers and Sanjay helps position Maya's chair at the table.

"It is tradition the birthday girl or boy cuts the cake." says Meta to Madison and Ethan, "Then cuts small pieces and serves each individually to every guest. Please, Madison." gesturing to her as Maya holds a small piece for her. Madison smiles as she takes the cake from Maya, followed by Ethan, who is on his very best behaviour.

Four hours later, the other guests have departed and Maya is sitting on the back patio with Madison and Ethan.

"This was my best birthday ever." Maya smiles at her friends. "It means so much that you are here."

"It was definitely the most interesting birthday I've ever been to." says Madison.

"I love your culture and traditions. I learned so

much. I meant to ask your Dad why he put that on your forehead?"

"Vermillion Tika is a powerful spiritual symbol. In astrology, the forehead is considered the seat of the "third eye" or the ajna chakra. This chakra is associated with intuition, perception, and spiritual awakening. Applying Vermillion Tika to this spot is believed to activate and energize the third eye, enhancing spiritual awareness. In astrology it is believed applying Vermillion Tika forms a protective barrier against negative energies and evil forces, keeping you safe from harm and negativity."

"That's fascinating." says Madison. "And could you explain the significance of the burning, uh, on the plate?"

"That is called Aarti, a sacred ritual in Hinduism that involves the offering of light and sound to deities, symbolizing devotion and seeking blessings. The rhythmic chants Ammi was doing creates a divine ambiance." Her phone pings and her lighthearted mood crashes. "I'm sorry, I have to make a call." Maya wheels away quickly and goes inside, leaving Madison and Ethan looking at each other.

A minute later Maya is on a Zoom with Khan and Courtnall, who are smiling on her monitor.

"Maya, we know it's your birthday but we had to call because we knew this would make your birthday even more special!" says Khan.

"We got the kids, Maya, all of them!" says Courtnall, wiping happy tears.

"Oh, my God, I can't believe it!" Maya shouts, hands to her face, as the tears begin.

"Maya, those kids will never know what you did for them, how much you cared about them, but the Prime Minister knows, and he asked us to tell you how grateful he is." says Khan, as Maya cries happy tears.

"I'm so, so happy for the children …for their families." wiping her tears.

"You go back to your party, Maya." smiles Khan.

"We promise we won't call you again tonight." says Courtnall, waving goodbye.

Maya shuts off her monitor. She wheels out of her office as the secret wall closes behind her. She opens her bedroom door and is greeted be four very worried faces. Meta quickly embraces her daughter.

"What's wrong dear? Can you tell us?" ending the embrace. Everyone is waiting on Maya. She smiles as she sniffs and wipes her eyes.

"I will never forget this birthday. This has been the best day of my life!"

Relief washes over the faces of her parents, and Madison and Ethan.

"I'm sorry I can't tell you about this call, but now I know, more than I ever have before, why I have been blessed with my special gifts."

Meta hugs her daughter tightly, both emotional. "I'm so proud of you." Then Sanjay hugs Maya. "Best birthday ever." he says.

"I'm so happy for you, Maya." says Madison, hugging her warmly.

"Let's have some cake to celebrate!" says Sanjay.

"That's a great idea!" Maya grins.

* * *

Next morning Mrs. G. is sitting on the living room sofa with Dr. G. having a DAC-chat with Madison and Ethan.

"Ethan wore one of Mr. Kumar's jackets. It's called a bandhgala. Everyone said he looked very handsome."

"I hope you got pictures?" says mom.

"Yes, Mr. Kumar's texting them to you."

Maya's bedroom overlooks the patio where Madison and Ethan are having their DAC-chat with mom and dad. The window is open enough so Maya can easily hear their conversation as she combs her hair, looking in her dresser mirror. But it's not as if she's eavesdropping.

"Did Dad tell you he sourced a place for us to buy luggage and clothes only a quarter mile from where we landed?" says Madison.

Maya scrunches up her face. *What is Madison talking about?* She's very curious as she quickly glides her wheelchair over to the window. She pulls back the curtain a few inches and peeks outside where she sees Madison and Ethan are seated on facing sofa chairs, six feet apart, where we saw them last night. They're having a conversation with their parents … *but neither of them are speaking with a phone*! Maya is so stunned she has to look away to gather herself. *How can they be talking to their parents without a phone? Only a quarter mile from where we landed. What's going on*?!

Sanjay and Meta are in the living room as Maya wheels inside moments later.

"Hi, dear. What are Madison and Ethan doing?" asks Meta.

"They're outside. Uh, papa, will you be driving them to the airport?"

"Yes, we'll be leaving in almost three hours."

"You said Dr. Giller asked you not to pick them up at the airport?"

"Yes, in case their connecting flight from Frankfurt was delayed. Why do you ask?"

"It's nothing. I'll be outside with Madison and Ethan." She wheels away, leaving her parents wondering what that was about.

Out on the Kumar's patio Madison and Ethan's DAC-chat continues.

"We'll be at the airport at 7:00 tonight and … oh, gotta go!" reacting to the back door opening and Maya glides out.

"I was just saying to Ethan it's so relaxing here in your garden." Madison smiles at Maya as she stops her wheelchair a few feet from the sofas. Maya's face is expressionless, looking at Madison, then at Ethan. Her guests are perplexed.

"Is there something wrong, Maya?" Madison asks.

"Did Dad tell you he sourced a place for us to buy luggage and clothes only a quarter mile from where we landed?"

Madison and Ethan are absolutely stunned, looking at each other. *Uh-oh*!

Moments later Maya looks more shocked than Madison and Ethan were minutes ago.

"Teleporting?" her brilliant mind trying to make sense of something so impossible to fathom. "This is like Star Wars science fiction!"

"I know. When dad told us, we were as stunned as you." grins Ethan.

"Your father lets you come so far alone?"

"We've ported several times with him and Mom." says Madison. "We had a great day in Paris, Rio de Janeiro and Waikiki and last month."
Maya looks at Ethan, then at Madison, like she's not sure she heard that right.

"You were in Paris, Rio de Janeiro and Waikiki *on the same day?"*
Madison and Ethan grin, almost embarrassed by it.

"I'm afraid to ask, but I need to know how long it took for you to come here from Florida?"

"About fifteen seconds." says Madison, looking at Maya, her mouth open. Then she begins to giggle.

"This is the most unbelievable thing I have ever heard, and yet I still can't believe it's true."

"I know, we still find it hard to believe." grins Ethan.

"Maya, you're dropping us at the airport at seven tonight." says Madison. "It will take us twenty minutes to taxi somewhere remote where we can safely. launch. When we get home - just after seven thirty your time - we'll call you."

"No, don't call then! We'll still be driving home." It takes a few seconds for it to register how *totally bizarre* that sounds, and then she starts to laugh. Madison and Ethan are so relieved this has turned out very well, much better than it could have. Maya wheels closer to Madison and speaks low.

"Could you please show me the HT?"

A few minutes later they're in Maya's bedroom, and Madison is demonstrating the cast-sleeve to Maya.

"Then we push a little button inside here, which activates this panel that slides open, giving us access to the HT."

"It's very similar to an iPhone." marvels Maya.

"Lunch is ready." Meta calls out from the hallway.

"Be right there, Ammi." she calls out reluctantly.

"We'll continue after we eat." says Madison.

"I will eat faster than I *ever have*." grins Maya.

Meta has prepared a delicious assortment of sandwiches and Shawarmas for lunch. Madison is seated beside Maya, quickly chewing a big mouthful. Ethan sits opposite beside Meta, and Sanjay is at the head of the table.

"I've never seen you eat so fast, Maya." says Meta.

"I'm hungrier than usual, and you know I love Shawarmas."

"What time will you arrive home tomorrow?" asks Sanjay, looking at Madison.
Maya chokes a little on her food, sneaking a quick look at Madison.

"You know, with the ten and a half hour time-change, I really don't know."

"I was saying to Mad', it's like we're going back in time, cuz' we've already been through Monday here." adds Ethan.

"Yes." grins Sanjay. "Save room for dessert, dear."

"I'll have it when we come home this evening."

Twenty minutes later Maya is back in her bedroom with Madison and Ethan. She has learned a lot about the HT, but wants to know more.

"Would you allow me to look inside the HT?

"I don't know if we should." says Madison.

"We've never seen the insides."

"I promise I won't break anything."
Madison looks at Ethan. He shrugs. Madison looks at Maya.

"Okay, but please don't take apart anything."

"Yeah, it'd be a bummer if Dad had to port here with a backup HT."

"And explain how he got here the same day." says Madison.

As Maya glides away from them the side wall slowly slides open. Madison and Ethan are very surprised to see the impressive workstation hidden behind.

"Maya? What's this?" asks Madison.

"My workstation." she shrugs, as if it's no big deal. "You showed me your secret, so I'm okay with you seeing where I do my work. But please don't ask me what I do, because I can't tell you. Ammi and papa don't even know."

"Okay." says Madison, then she looks at Ethan. Wow!

Maya very carefully takes the HT device from inside the cast-sleeve. She checks how the back panel is secured, and it only takes her a minute to have the insides of the HT exposed. Maya looks closely at the hardware.

"During my post-graduate studies I spent two semesters researching the probability of humans teleporting in the next twenty-five years."

"Really?" says Madison. "What did you conclude?"

"I am convinced it will happen. Your father solved the biggest challenge with the body neutralizing pill. It's astounding he accomplished that on his own."

"He's pretty amazing." says Ethan.

"Now that he's done this, I'd love to know if he's working on teleporting back in time." continuing to look at the hardware.

"You mean like those silly movies where someone goes back in time and does the opposite of what they did years earlier and they live happily ever after?" says Madison.

"No, I'm thinking about the people who rob banks, kill people, kidnap kids, and the police have no leads. If the Police could teleport back even just 24 hours and witness the crime being committed, they could rescue the victims and arrest the bad guys."

"It sounds great, but I don't see it happening in our lifetime." says Madison.

Maya looks at her. "Why not? Ethan, did your father allow you to review his research?"

"Yes, except for what's in the BNG pill."

"He doesn't want us to know for security reasons." says Madison.

"I don't need to know. But I'd love to see your father's research papers."

"We couldn't do that, Maya." Madison says.

"Why is it so important?" asks Ethan.

Maya looks away, wrestling with a thought. After a moment, "I need you to promise you will never tell anyone what I'm going to tell you."

Madison looks at Ethan. They nod.

"We promise, Maya." says Madison.

"Bring those chairs." Maya asks Ethan, who quickly drags two chairs over. They sit down, looking intently at Maya.

"After I won the IT Competition my mother and father were contacted by a man who works for our government's Intelligence Agency. They had learned I was very good at breaking encrypted codes, deciphering cryptic e-mails and things like that. The man told my parents they needed me to be able to work for them when they had something very important that maybe only I could do. My parents and I agreed, because it would help my country and our citizens."

Madison and Ethan are impressed. Maya continues.

"The government provided me with this work station and these very powerful computers. Two nights ago when my phone beeped after dinner, it was the Intelligence people. They only contact me when it is something critically important. They have been trying to arrest some people who have harmed many people for many months. They got a lead just before they called me. They needed me to decrypt an e-mail they had intercepted which provided very valuable information."

She turns on her computer and one of her two monitors. Madison and Ethan watch as Maya quickly makes some keystrokes and now on the monitor the screen is divided into four squares with video of vehicles on highways and streets. The city

name appears above each square; New York.
London. Mumbai. Rome.

"What's this?" asks Ethan.

"Live video from those four cities. They needed me to hack into the video of a highway in a city that I can't mention, and replay the video from two days earlier to try to locate a suspicious vehicle. The work I did that night resulted in many lives being saved - I can't provide any details - which was why I was so emotional last night … it was the first time my work had such meaningful results."

"It's incredible you're doing this kind of work, Maya."says Madison. "My mind is totally blown." says Ethan.

"Thank you. The work is very frustrating because there are so many cases where we have very little evidence. Now do you see why in my wildest dreams I wish we could go back in time? Your father's HT could save the lives of so many people."

"I totally get it, Maya, but he would never allow your government or the Police to access the HT." says Madison.

"Why?"

"He's afraid the technology will get in the wrong hands." says Ethan.

"He wants to keep it secret until after he dies." says Madison.

"What?!" Maya gasps. "That could be *forty* years! God willing."

"I'm sorry, Maya." says Madison. "Dad won't agree."
Maya sighs.

At 6:55 that evening the Departures Zone at Maharaj International Airport is busy with travellers exiting vehicles. Sanjay and Meta are standing next to their Van, watching Madison and Ethan say their goodbyes to Maya, thirty feet away.

"We'll see you soon, Maya." says Madison.

"Now that you know we're just around the corner." Ethan grins. Maya smiles.

"We'll call you later." They hug.

"Remember … wait *at least an hour* until I get home."
They all chuckle.

* * *

9. THEIR INSPIRATION

Mom and Dad are having breakfast with Madison and Ethan, looking at the photos Mr. Kumar took at Maya's birthday party.

"I love that jacket!" says mom, seeing the orange jacket Maya let Madison wear.

"Her closet is a rainbow of colors! Hardly a grey or black for that girl." smiles Madison, wearing a yellow hoodie and jeans.

"Oh, Ethan, you look so handsome!" says mom, looking at a photo of him in Mr. Kumar's white bandhgala with many red flowers and plants.

"Yeah, well don't go buying me one." he says.

"It's so nice to see you with your hair combed." grins mom.

"That's what I told him!" grins Madison.

"Don't get used to it." he says through a yawn.

"You must be exhausted." says dad.

"Yeah, the circadian's really messed up." he says.

"I'm so happy you've made a new friend." says mom.

"Sanjay told me they haven't seen Maya this happy in years."

"That's great." says Madison. "Okay, we have to

get to class. Great seeing you, Mom. Safe porting."
they hug. "Love you."

It's two-thirty on a cloudy afternoon in Majorca, and
dozens of Police Officers have assembled in a
schoolyard. They are joined today by the twenty
remaining candidates in the Cadet Training
Program, but it's not a celebration. They are
gathered with dozens of people from the community,
and TV and radio reporters, to hear an update on a
case that has rocked their community. Police Chief
Eduardo Nunez stands near a large poster with a
color photo of a beautiful girl, eight years old. The
name "MARIA" is printed below with several red
hearts around it. Chief Nunez is speaking to the
subdued throng.

"Today is day five since Maria was taken from her
bed. Our Officers have been working tirelessly to
find Maria and bring her home to her family."
Rafael shakes his head sadly, as Chief Nunez
continues. "Today I am very grateful to welcome
twenty men presently in our cadet training course
who requested they be permitted to join our search
team." He claps his hands, and the crowd joins in
the brief applause.

Ninety minutes later Rafael is walking in a heavily
wooded area with several of his fellow Cadets, all
wearing a yellow flak-jacket vest. The men are
spaced ten feet apart to maximize the coverage area.
They're looking closely towards the rough terrain,

looking for a footprint, a torn piece of clothing, anything that could be evidence in Maria's kidnapping. The Cadet on Rafael's right speaks without taking his gaze from the ground.

"I can't imagine what the parents are going through. Their only child." They walk on..

* * *

Madison and Ethan are walking into school as Rebecca and Natalie come over.

"Hey, Mad' .. E'." says Rebecca, sporting a pink hoodie and jeans. "How was Palo Alto?" pronouncing it like the guys' name Paolo.

"It was good."

"What'd you do?" asks Natalie.

"Uh, went to the Zoo and a friend's birthday party."

"You didn't post anything yet?"asks Rebecca.

"The family doesn't do social."

"Seriously?" says Rebecca.

"Are they in witness protection?" grins Natalie, and Rebecca laughs.

"Not everyone's on social." as she and her BFF's enter their classroom, and Ethan walks on.

"Hey, E'." best friend Garret walks up. "How was your weekend?"

"It was okay. We went to the Zoo … and a birthday party."

"Palo Alto has a Zoo?"

"Uh, not sure." says Ethan, thinking quickly, "we went to Frisco."

"You really get around, man." grins Garret. Ethan shrugs. *If you only knew.*

Rafael has just showered after his long day in the woods searching for clues in Maria's disappearance. He pulls a yellow t-shirt over his wet hair, leaving it un-tucked over his dark jeans. He looks tired as he grabs a towel and vigorously rubs the moisture from his long, black hair. He runs his fingers through his hair and is fastening it into a ponytail when his phone pings on the night table. He picks it up. A text from Madison. *2 late 2 chat?* A flicker of a smile creases his face. He hesitates a moment. Then he types and sends. In seconds his phone rings and then he's looking at the smiling faces of Madison and Ethan.

"Hey, Madison, Ethan, how are you?" with not his normal big smile.

"Great." says Ethan.

"Glad we didn't leave it too late to call." says Madison.

"I'm really glad you did. I needed to see your smiles." his sadness clear.

"Please don't tell us they cut you from training?" says Madison.

"No, everything is good, thanks." he sniffs.

"Is it your papa?" Madison asks, very concerned.

"No, he is good, thank you." he takes a big breath

and exhales. "So, uh, five days ago this little girl" he holds her photo for them to see, "her name is Maria, she was taken from her bedroom in the nighttime not far from here. She's eight years old, and there's been a massive search for her .. police .. friends .. the whole community, but there were very few clues."

Madison and Ethan are stone-faced, afraid to speak.

"There was no ransom demand .. her family is not wealthy. Maria's their only child, and they've been praying for her on TV every day. We asked if we could join the search team today." He takes a breath, as Madison looks at Ethan, both very moved by his story.

"And uh, two hours ago we found her…" he stops and lowers his head, emotional. Madison's eyes are wet with tears. For a little girl she never knew, who she now realizes is not coming home to her family. And for the pain her friend is feeling. Ethan hands her a tissue. Rafael looks at his screen and sees Madison's tears, and Ethan's sad face.

"I'm sorry, guys. I should let you go." wiping his eyes.

"No, we'll stay with you as long as you need us." says Madison.

Moments later their tears have stopped, but not their emotions.

"Her parents checked on her when they went to bed at midnight. Three hours hours later they were awakened by noises and Maria was gone. Their doorbell camera was broken so Police had no video, but they're certain she was taken when the noises awakened her parents."

"I can't imagine losing your only child that way." Madison says softly.

"She had her whole life ahead of her. Her mama said she loved soccer, painting and making cupcakes." He swallows hard, then looks away.

"When my mama died I didn't understand fully that I would never see her again. I was so sad .. and very angry. Why would God take my mama from me. One day papa sat me down .. he said 'Rafael, if mama could come back for just one minute to speak with you, I know she would hold you so tight and tell you she had a special favor to ask you to do for her. I asked papa what would mama ask. He said it would make mama so happy if she could watch me every day from Heaven being happy, not being sad, just remembering the good times we had, and how much she loved me. I said I didn't know if I could do it, because I was so sad. Papa said he was very sad, too, but we had to try because mama was watching us, looking over us. It was so hard, but … it's what got us through it." He looks away for a moment, then -

"I know it will be a very long time before Maria's papa and mama can be happy … …"
Madison is tissuing tears. He looks at his friends' stoic faces.

"I really appreciate you staying with me, guys."

"I'm glad we could be here for you." says
Madison.

"Get some sleep, man. Call us tomorrow, okay?"
says Ethan.

"I will. 'Night, guys." and his screen goes blank.

Madison closes her laptop and looks at him.

"What a beautiful little girl … her whole life
ahead of her."

"Yeah …"

"Her eyes .. that smile. So innocent … so much
love." She closes her eyes.

"Can I get you anything?" he asks softly.
Madison opens her eyes and reaches her arms out.
He gives her a big hug.

The next morning a video is playing on
Madison's laptop. It's Maria's mama, speaking to the
media a few days ago when hope for Maria's safe
return still filled her heart. Her husband beside her,
standing next to the big poster of Maria we saw
yesterday.

"We are begging you, whoever you are, please
don't harm our Maria, she is our only child.
Please, just let her go, we will not bring charges
against you, we just need our baby to come home."
then she breaks down, sobbing into her husband's
arms. Madison closes her computer.

"That's awful." says dad. "A parent's worst

nightmare. Rafael's a good man. I feel bad for him, but that's the career he's chosen."

"I could never do that job. I'd bring it home with me." says Madison.

"Me, too." says Ethan.

"You've never been in a fight." says dad, grinning.

"Yeah, and I hope I never am."

* * *

The *Rebels* practice is almost over and Coach Jamieson isn't pleased. She blows her whistle a little longer than usual, telling her charges this stoppage won't be good. "Bring it in!" Coach snaps, and the tired, sweaty girls jog over faster than usual.

"Someone please finish this sentence for me … We .. play .. like .. we …"

"Practice." Madison says, not looking at Coach.

"Right! And in my eleven years coaching, *that* has always proven true! We're playing to win our first Conference Championship in fourteen years in two weeks, but if we play like this …!" She looks at her watch. "I need to get you focused … you won't need the ball."
Madison looks at Rebecca, they know what this is.

Ten minutes later the *Rebels* have been running sprints, in two groups of seven, from the goal line to mid-field and back, twice, for nine minutes. Madison and Rebecca are sucking air, hands on knees.

"Somethin' crawled up …" gasping, "her butt, huh?" says Rebecca.

"Who knows." Madison gasps, wiping sweat from her forehead, as the whistle blows, their signal to begin another sprint. Madison runs off with Rebecca.

Later Coach Jamieson is walking off the pitch with Madison. "Bec, Nat', and you weren't sharp today."

"Yeah, one of those days."

"Everything good at home?"

There's some things I'll never be able to tell you. Like a little girl I can't stop thinking about.

"Yeah, thanks."

"I know you'll be ready in two weeks. Make sure 'Bec and Nat' are."

"Count on it, Coach."

At ten o'clock that evening Madison is laying on her bed, on a Zoom with Maya, where it's eight-thirty the next morning in Mumbai.

"I'm working from home today, so I thought I'd call before you sleep, see how you and Ethan are."

"That's so nice of you, Maya." her energy and smile wattage below normal, which Maya notices.

"Is everything okay?" a little concerned.

"No …."

Madison told Maya about Rafael, and the tragedy of Maria's death -

"The death of a child is a tragedy, but it is horrific in cases like Maria."

"Rafael was so distraught, Maya, and he'd never met her."

"That tells me he is a good man with a big heart. You and Ethan didn't know Maria, yet you are also feeling a deep loss."

"I'll never forget her, she was so precious. I can't explain it."

"I can."

"Please tell me."

"In Hindu dharma the Sanskrit words Vasudhaiva Kutumbakam means the world is one family. When every human being is born he or she is now part of one universe, one consciousness, based on an ancient belief of oneness, a sense of belongingness to all others. Vasudhaiva means earth, and so this belief is one of having compassion for all people on earth."

"That's beautiful, Maya. Thank you so much for sharing."

"Of course. In my work with the Agency I also experience a deep connection with the victims we are trying to save, though I realize we will never meet."

"We saw that! You were overwhelmed!"

"I was, and from that day I have been at peace - it is just as stressful - but now I know I am doing the work I am supposed to be doing."

"That's great, Maya. I'm so happy for you."

"Thanks, Madison. Uh, could you please send me Maria's photo?"

"Yeah … sure." a little surprised, but pleased.

"Thanks. Sleep well, my friend." she smiles, hand over her heart.

"You, too. Uh, I mean, have a great day, Maya." she smiles, hand over her heart.

Madison closes her laptop and puts it on the night table. Then she walks out of her room, as Dad is walking up the stairs.

"Is E' home yet?"

"Yeah .. he's on the deck."

Ethan's on the two-seater sofa, mom and dad's fave deck spot, looking at the big Moon shining brightly. Dark hoodie pulled over his light hair that hasn't seen a comb since Maya's birthday. As Madison walks out she feels the cool air on her cheeks and pulls her sky blue hoodie over her dark hair. She's got a bag of just opened nachos that brings a smile to his face and his hands out of the warmth of his hoodie pockets.

"Readin' my mind." snaring two. "Look how close the Moon's tonight. Seems like you could drive two blocks, grab a step ladder and climb on it."

"Why is that?" sitting beside him.

"Dad says when it's near the horizon the ground and horizon make it seem close. It's got to do with how our brain calculates size-distance ratios with changes in the light … it makes it appear larger, ergo, closer."

"It's really amazing people have walked on it."

"Yeah, me and Garret often think about the people who told the Wright brothers they were crazy."

"Yeah, really. How long was their first flight?"

"Fifty-nine seconds … 859 feet."

"It must have been an unbelievable feeling."

"I can only imagine. Too bad Wilbur didn't live to see how big it became."

"What happened?"

"He got typhoid fever nine, ten years later. I think he was forty-five."

"That's sad. How long did his brother live?"

"Another thirty years or so."

"By then flying was pretty routine, right?"

"Oh, yeah."

"Think they ever imagined people would go to the moon?"

"I doubt it, not way back then."

"They'd be blown away if they could see the world today."

"Oh, yeah. Satellites … GPS." grabs another nacho. "The Space Station."

"Yeah." grabs a nacho. "So, Maya just called."

"Oh, how's she doin'?"

"Good. She's working from home today. I told her about Maria."

"She must see a lot of cases like that, huh?"

"She does. She told me something really profound …"

After telling Ethan what Maya had shared with her -

"It made me think. The HT will likely have more impact on the world than Neil Armstrong walking on the Moon, and forty years is a very long time, E'." Ethan stops chewing his nacho and looks at his sister.

"You want to let Maya look at Dad's research papers?" he whispers, stunned.

"Yes, but on one condition." whispering. "She absolutely swears if she finds a way to teleport back in time, she *can't tell anyone*, unless dad approves." Ethan leans closer to her, whispering lower, and more firmly.

"Mad', he'll never agree, and he'd be sooo angry with us! No, no way!"

"But if he knew it could save the lives of little girls like Maria, maybe he'd see it differently. It's worth a try, E'!"

"You know how bad I feel that Maya knows! Now you want me to share Dad's research with someone we just met?"

"We didn't betray Dad. It was an accident. And I really believe she was meant to find out." looking closely at him. "E', what if the Wright brothers had given up? What if that meant man didn't land on the Moon until forty years later?"

Ethan turns away and looks at the Moon for fifteen seconds. It feels like fifteen minutes for Madison. He turns to face her and leans close.

"Okay … but it was *your* idea … and I didn't want to do it."
Madison is so excited! She raises her right hand with baby finger extended. He follows and they do the *pinkie swear.*

"Thanks, E'! This is so exciting! she grins, hugging him.
But it's clear he doesn't share her enthusiasm.

10. THE FIRST STEP

"We'll be home by ten-thirty, dear." says Meta, kissing Maya on the cheek.

"Are you going to watch a little TV?" asks Sanjay.

"I may after I finish some paperwork. Have fun." Meta and Sanjay exit the house, leaving the big wooden door open, where Maya watches them get in their SUV and drive away. Maya quickly closes the door and locks it. Then she reverses her wheelchair and begins to move along the hallway floor, looking very excited.

There's a big, metal shed in the Kumar's backyard. Kneeling behind it, hidden by a few leafy bushes, are Madison and Ethan, just arrived from their latest *flight*. Peering through the bushes they can see Maya has just come outside and is scanning the grounds for any sign of them. Maya whistles a two-syllable refrain, which is their cue they're clear to appear. Seeing them walk out from behind the shed brings a huge smile to Maya's face.

"I'm so excited to see you." as Madison and Ethan jog up and lean in for warm hugs.

"It's so good to see you, Maya." Madison says.

"How was your *flight*, Ethan?" she grins.

"Successful .. and very fast." he grins.

"Let's get inside before any neighbors see you."

Two minutes later Maya is at her workstation, flipping through a thick stack of papers.

"There is so much to review."

"Take all the time you need." says Ethan.

"But only in here." cautions Madison.

"Of course."

"If you have any questions, just shoot me a generic text." says Ethan.

"I only do cryptic. If I need you to answer a question, I'll text …, um, *it's very cloudy here today. I bet it's always sunny in Florida.*"

"Very cool." grins Ethan.

"Can you stay for awhile? I have two hours."

"Wish we could, but we need to get home for breakfast." says Madison.

"Okay. Could I watch you teleport?" she smiles eagerly.

Madison and Ethan are kneeling behind the shed in the Kumar's backyard. Maya is in her wheelchair, looking left, then right.

"There's no one outside or looking out windows." she advises. Madison and Ethan breathe in deeply and then forcefully exhale, as Maya watches, mesmerized. Then they quickly press the Launch key … and a second later, they have vanished!

Maya is astounded. It's one thing to hear about such an incredible feat, but to actually witness it right in front of you? Maya looks to the dark skies and starts to giggle. Seconds later she's gliding along the paved walkway towards the back door when her phone *Pings.* She chuckles as she stops, takes out her phone and looks at the screen. *'Great'* with an *Airplane* emoji. Maya grins and composes a reply. *Show off*! She sends the text and looks up to the sky.

* * *

Two weeks later Madison is in the kitchen making her smoothie. A pink hoodie covers her hair. White shorts, bare feet. As the blender roars, she's leaning against the island, looking with a fixed gaze towards the floor, like she's deep in thought about something. Ethan walks in, dressed as usual - yellow T-, faded jeans with a few tears, ball cap and runners - but absent this morning is his usual carefree vibe. He looks at Madison twenty feet away but she doesn't look up. He goes to the blender and turns it off. He grabs a glass and fills it, puts it on the table and walks to his sister.

"You got this, Mad'." putting his hands on her shoulders. She snaps out of it.

"I know." with the hint of a smile.

That afternoon the stands at Walker Field are packed mostly with Walker High students and parents, and a few dozen Lakefield supporters. They're here for the Championship match, which would be the first for the *Rebels* in fourteen years. There's also over a dozen coaches and staff from the top NCAA universities' soccer Programs here to watch one of the State's top players. As she warms-up, Madison recognizes many of the faces who have been coming to some of her matches this year to scout her in advance of her upcoming Senior year. She's flattered by the attention, but it doesn't faze her because it's pretty much a done deal that she's going to Stanford in sixteen months.

Sitting among the *Rebels* supports are Dr. G. and Mrs. G, who arrived from Palo Alto fifteen minutes after her morning lecture finished.

"Mad' looks locked in, dear." says mom.

"She does." says Dr. G.

Two hours later the *Rebels* Field scoreboard fills Ethan's phone camera as he does his in-match commentary for an exclusive audience of two.

"With two minutes left in extra time in the Championship match the score is tied at two. Madison's been the star of the game, scoring both *Rebels* goals. Lakefield players seem to be feeling the effects of the humid temps today in Merritt Island. They will certainly be keying on Madison in these final, tense minutes. Let's watch." he grins. "You know, Maya, this is so much fun, maybe I will change my major to sports broadcasting?""

There's an injury timeout and *Rebels* Coach Jamieson is with her players.

"They're running on fumes, guys! Let's take it to them!" clapping her hands, exhorting the girls for a final push.

The Referee blows her whistle and play resumes with the *Rebels* bringing the ball down field. Natalie makes a short pass to Madison, running slowly, assessing her next play. The defender covering Rebecca stumbles and Madison seizes on the small opening, chipping a nice leading pass to Rebecca. Just like they did in the previous playoff game, Rebecca stops on a dime, causing her defender to lose a step, which gives Rebecca that extra second to loft a delicate pass to a streaking Madison. She covers the ball without breaking stride and when she's thirty feet from the keeper a lunging defender slides into Madison just as she was about to make a clear strike. Madison falls to the ground grabbing her left ankle. The Referee signals a penalty kick and Mad's' teammates help her to her feet, grimacing.

"You good, Mad'?" asks Rebecca, wiping the sweat from her face.

"No broken bones." getting to her feet and testing the ankle.

Up in the stands Dr. G. and Mrs. G. are standing among the 200 fans. "Mad's' got a penalty kick to win the Championship, Gordon!"

Madison takes her position for the penalty kick. With a steely-eyed focus she stares down the keeper who's bouncing on her toes, left-right, left-right. Madison moves to make the strike with her right foot. But she stops in mid-motion, her foot not two feet from the ball. The keeper is in mid-air, diving to her left where she is certain the ball is going. Madison calmly rights herself and kicks the ball into the wide open goal as the helpless keeper makes a valiant lunge to get back, but she's not even close. The ecstatic *Rebels* mob a happy Madison.

"Way to go, Mad!" .. "You did it!" .. "Amazing!"

Moments later the game is over and Ethan is grinning ear-to-ear, filming himself.

"What a performance! Madison scored all three goals to lead the *Rebels* to their first Conference championship in fourteen years."

Fifteen feet away his parents watch the *Rebels* celebrate. "She came through with the championship on the line, Gordon!" as Madison jogs over, smiling broadly.

"I'm so proud of you, Mad'!"

"Thanks, Mom." hugging her, then dad.

"Great match, dear."

"Thanks, Dad. Glad you were both here."

Rebecca and Natalie jog up.

"Congratulations Bec' and Nat', you both played great."

"Thanks, Mrs. G." says Rebecca. "Did you get some great vid for your uncle, E'?"

"Oh, yeah, he's gonna love it." he grins.

The following morning Madison and Ethan are in her bedroom on a laptop Zoom with Maya, who is smiling broadly.

"I felt like I was right there! It was so exciting! How did you manage to keep your composure?"

"It takes a lot of practice. Having trust in my ability."

"Ammi and papa asked me to give you their congratulations."

"Thanks, Maya. Please give them my best."

"So, uh, how's *it* going? Ethan asks, which instantly crashes the fun vibe.

"I wish I had good news. I'm still struggling to solve the next step …"

"It must be very frustrating." says Madison.

"It is, but I'm not giving up. I still have hope. I'm certain your father had many obstacles to overcome to develop it."

"It took him two years." says Ethan.

"I believe what he created is more difficult than my challenge, so I have to believe I will discover a solution."

"We're praying for you." Madison says.

"Thanks." Maya smiles with a little wave.

Madison closes her laptop and looks at Ethan.

"What are you thinking?

"I've got mixed feelings. It'd be incredible if she found a way to do it, but…"

"Then we have to tell Dad." finishing what she knows is troubling him.

"Yeah …"

"It could be months before we need to have that conversation."

"*We*?" he semi-grins. "*You'll* be telling him." he puts his arm around her shoulders. "I'm gonna show him the bruises on my back from you beating me to get me to agree." he grins, and she laughs.

* * *

11. RAFAEL'S BIG DAY!

Rafael's Papa is in his Sunday best sitting proudly in the third row of seating for the families of the twelve men being sworn in today as members of the Palma Police Force. Papa is filming the ceremony on his phone, and he stands now for a better view as Rafael, in a black suit, white shirt and black tie, walks up to the Police Chief to receive his Certificate and pose for photos.

Later, Rafael and Papa are having a quiet moment sitting at a table at a reception for the new Officers.

"I wish Mama was here, she would be so proud, Rafael."

"Thanks, Papa."

"I am happy now with your decision. You are a very good mechanic, but you will do more good helping people."

"Yes, I believe that." he nods. "Did you get some good video?"

"Oh, yes." he smiles.

"I need to get someone to do one more video." looking around.

Majorca is six hours ahead of Merritt Island, so Rafael's text pings as Madison and Ethan are having breakfast with dad.

"It's Rafael. Oh, there's a video." Madison says excitedly.

"He's graduating today." Ethan says to dad as Madison holds her phone for them to watch. Rafael is smiling, standing with his papa.

"Hello my good friends in Merritt Island, Florida. This is a very proud and happy day for me. I want you to meet my Papa and best friend, we're celebrating with my fellow graduates and their families. And I want to congratulate you Madison on winning the Championship. You played amazing! I really enjoyed your video, Ethan, thanks very much! And give my best to your mom and dad, please. Okay we have to go, talk soon, guys." he smiles and the video ends.

"I'm so happy for him." she says.

"Great day for him and his papa." says dad.

"Okay, have a good one." getting up. He kisses Madison on the cheek and fist bumps Ethan.

"You too, Dad." says Madison. She grabs her phone and begins to compose a text.

Back at Rafael's reception he's with his Papa when his phone pings. He looks at the screen; Madison's text; *Congratulations Rafael! We're very happy for you! Great to meet your papa. Let's talk tomorrow.* He smiles.

The following afternoon Madison and Ethan are on the two-seater on the deck, on a Zoom with Rafael.

"When do you start?" Madison asks.

"Next week. I've been assigned to a veteran officer."

"We're really happy for you." says Ethan.

"Thanks. So, what's up next for you guys?"

"Finals to write and then I start my camp counsellor job." says Madison.

"What kind of camp is it?"

"Boys and girls ages seven to twelve. Teaching them soccer and other sports. It's my second summer. I love it."

"That's great. What about you, Ethan?"

"Finals .. an' me an' Garrett have a landscaping business. Cut lawns, trim hedges."

"Amazing! When did you start doing that?"

"About two years ago. We have nine clients now, and they're all close by."

"That's very impressive. Okay, I have to get going. I'll call you next weekend."

"Have a great first week, Rafael." the screen goes blank.

* * *

Over the next eight weeks Madison was enjoying her work at the Camp. It was six days a week, so she didn't really feel like porting off to faraway locales with the family every Sunday. Ethan and Garrett's business would be ideal if they could do three lawns a day and take four days off, but they have to do the work when the client requests it, which usually has them working five or six days a week. Despite this work schedule Madison and Ethan had made three clandestine trips to Mumbai on Sunday mornings, when it was around midnight here. Each visit was right after they received this text; *"it's very cloudy today."* Her hacker skills are world-class and she knows there's others with similar talents lurking on the Dark Web with criminal intent looking for data to steal and sell for big bucks. That's why she refused to express her questions to Madison and Ethan via text or e-mail, knowing if they were ever intercepted it would be disastrous.

Madison loves being around young kids and hopes to have a bunch herself one day. She's sharing her knowledge today with a dozen kids sitting on the grass.

"Feeling nervous before and during a game is natural. Who can tell me why?"
A ten year old boy with a buzz cut and freckles raises his hand.

"Yes, Oliver?"

"So, uh, I get really nervous when I have to do a penalty kick."

"Very good answer, Oliver. Why do you get nervous?"

"Because I know everybody's looking at me."

"That's right. I used to really tense up and most times I flubbed the shot. I'd get so upset. Then my Mom taught me about visualization."

"What's that, Madison?" Oliver asks.

"You concentrate really hard with your eyes closed, maybe lying in bed, and imagine you're playing a game and you have to take that penalty kick. You focus really hard on being right there on the pitch, staring at the keeper. You know they're just as nervous as you, right?"
The kids all nod their heads, as Madison continues.

"I did this every night at bedtime when I was nine that winter. I bet I did five hundred imaginary kicks, and when the next soccer season started and I had my first penalty kick I wasn't nearly as nervous. Can anyone tell me why?"

"Because you did five hundred penalty kicks in your head during the winter?"

"That's right, Oliver. I was practising, even though I wasn't playing."

"I'm gonna try that, Madison!" grins Oliver.

"I am too!" shout the other kids.
Madison loves their energy. Her phone *pings*. She takes it out. It's a text from Maya. But it's not "*it's very cloudy today*" like the last bunch. This text has a bunch of '*Sunshine*' emojis and reads: *today is THE BEST*! *Wish you were here to enjoy it with me*! With a dozen *thumbs up* emojis. Madison is stunned. "She's done it!" barely audible.

12. GOIN' BACK IN TIME!

Madison received Maya's text just before lunch on Saturday, which was almost ten-thirty in the evening in Mumbai. Even if she and Ethan weren't working, it was far too risky to port to Mumbai then because Meta and Sanjay would either be in bed, or about to. They had no choice but to wait. Tomorrow was Sunday and Maya texted them later with a cryptic message; *Ammi and papa going to Temple 11:00 a.m. I can't go.* With a *sad face* emoji. Now they knew they were *porting* to Mumbai at thirty minutes after midnight tonight! The wait was agonizing for them, so they decided to kill some time and watch a film. But not just *any* film … it was one they'd never watched until three months ago, because they didn't like *silly* stories where the hero time-travels to alter the course of his life. *As if that could ever happen!* Now they were watching the Michael J. Fox classic *Back To The Future* for the ninth time since Maya began studying their dad's research papers.

"Whatcha watching?" dad says cheerily, walking into the living room.

"Back To The Future." says Madison casually.

"Classic film! Watched it fifty times." sitting down. "Oh, this scene is so funny!"

"No spoiler alerts!" chimes in Ethan.

"Okay, I promise." smiling at them.

An hour later Madison is stuffing pillows and sweaters under her bedsheets in the form of a body. She finishes and checks out her work. *Yeah, that looks like I'm sleeping.* She turns out the lights and opens her door and tip-toes to Ethan's closed bedroom door. She softly taps once and he opens it. His room is dark. She looks towards his bed at the similar 'body' he's created. She gives him a thumbs up. They tip-toe out and go down the stairs. When they get on the deck they look at that big piece of cheese that looks so close you think you could …

"That's a really good omen, Mad'. he whispers. She nods, excited.

* * *

Two minutes later Madison and Ethan are 8,800 hundred miles away, standing beside Maya's workstation, busting with excitement to hear what Maya has to report.

"I'm ninety-nine per cent certain you can do it."

"We can really go back in time?" says Madison, eyes wide.

"How many hours?" asks Ethan.

"My calculations are based on going back up to twenty-four."

"How do you do that without working on the hardware?" he asks.

"It's the data I input that determines the result."

"Where do you get it?" Madison asks.

"From metadata, algorithms, coding, it's incredibly complicated because I needed to unlock several firewalls to gain access to each step."

"This is unbelievable, E!" looking at her brother.

"Have you seen the film Back To The Future?" he asks.

"Of course! At least twenty-five times!"

"But this is totally different." says Madison.

"Yeah, you're not using a Delorean." Maya grins.

"Are you ready for us to test it?" Madison asks.

"Yes."

"Okay, I'll go, E'."

"No, I should go."

"Why?"

"Because if there's a technical problem, I'm more qualified to fix it."

"What do you mean?" Maya asks.

"What if I can't return to the present time?"

"You mean, like ever?" asks Madison.

"Why would that be a problem? You're not going back to when you were babies." Maya says.

"So if we could never come back to present time, no one would ever know?"

"It's only a few hours, Ethan, how would they?"

"Right." he nods. "Okay, so we go back ten hours to witness a crime, tell us what happens."

"You'll be across the street hiding behind a big bush or garbage bin watching the bad guys when they did the robbery. You'll get video with your video glasses and your Drone Bird. Did you bring them?

"Yes, and our digital audio chips." says Ethan.

"Good. Okay, I found a good test for you." turning on her computer.

"Uh, it's not gonna be a robbery, right?" asks Madison.

"Oh, no, don't worry." Maya smiles.

Madison looks at Ethan. Both excited.

Twenty minutes later Madison and Ethan have ported back eighteen hours to an alleyway off a busy street in downtown Mumbai. They pull their hoodies over their heads, put on their video glasses, and walk out to the street. Madison looks at a digital clock across the street showing the time is 12:32.

"It's happening in one minute." says Madison.

"Let's test our DAC's. Go over there thirty feet." Ethan jogs over. "Testing, 1-2-3." Madison says.

"Loud and clear, Mad'." says Ethan.

"Can you hear me, Maya?" is met by silence.

"Testing, testing, 1-2-3 … Maya?"

"Maybe she can't hear us cuz' we've gone back in time."

"Shhh!" cautions Madison, looking around.

Ethan points behind Madison. "This may be it .. the light just turned red." Madison turns around. A yellow SUV that was stopped at the intersection for a red light, begins to drive north. A black truck driving west doesn't stop for the red light and crashes into the right, rear side of the SUV. People rush to the vehicles. Madison looks at Ethan and they speak low, but very excited.

"Mad, we did it!!!" grinning, he hugs her. "We just took the first video of something that happened *yesterday*!"

"Shhh, people might hear you." she cautions, grinning.

"I can't help it, this is historical!!"

"I can't wait to see Maya, she'll be ecstatic!"

Two minutes later Maya wheels inside her home and Ethan closes the back door. They've been holding their emotions in check until they got inside and now they scream loudly, hugging each other.

"You did it, Maya!!" Madison says.

"Now we know how the Wright brothers must have felt!" grins Ethan.

"It was no different than our other flights, Maya!"

"You don't feel any different physically?"

"No, not yet, anyway." says Madison, as Ethan shakes his head.

"Monitor any changes in how you feel for the next few days." Maya cautions.

"So you didn't hear us say testing 1-2-3?" as they move down the hallway.

"Not when you're back in time. I can't wait to see your video." gliding into her bedroom and activating the sliding wall.

"I'll send it when I get at home." says Ethan.

"I can hack into it your computer in two minutes." Maya scoffs like it's easy-peasy. Minutes later, video of the car accident plays on one of Maya's monitors. Her second monitor is playing video of Madison, taken from Ethan's video glasses.

"Mad, we did it!!! We just took the first video of something that happened *yesterday*!

"Shhh, people might hear you."

"I can't help it, this is historical!!"

"I can't wait to see Maya!! She'll be ecstatic!" and the video ends.

"You have to delete this, Maya." says Madison. Maya's fingers flash across the keyboard.

"Deleted. Never to be seen again."

"You're a thousand per cent certain?"

"I can't guarantee a distant civilization a billion miles away …" smiling. "But the more important question is, how will you tell your Dad?"

"E' and I have plan." looking at her brother. Suddenly, there's a noise from down the hall, followed by voices. Maya is stunned!

"They're home an hour early!" she whispers to her friends. She quickly takes out her phone and composes a text.

In the living room Sanjay assists Meta, who appears to be in some discomfort.

"Let's get you comfortable." getting her seated in a comfy chair. "I'll get some water." As he walks, his phone pings and he takes it out. He looks at the screen; *CODE RED*! He looks down the hall. The light above Maya's door is RED.

In Maya's bedroom, the teens' conversation is hushed.

"They know Code Red means I'm in a critical operation and must never be disturbed, unless it is life and death." whispers Maya.

"We have to get home before Dad wakes up!" says Madison.
Maya motions to follow her. When they get to the bedroom door they listen intently for any sound. Only her father's muffled voice, still in the front room. Maya motions to follow as she glides to her windows and whispers to them. Ethan slowly slides open the ground floor window and peeks his head out a few inches. He looks at them and nods. He hugs Maya and they watch him climb out the window. Madison hugs Maya and she follows her brother. Maya watches them dash behind the shed.

In the living room, Sanjay is tending to Meta as Maya glides into the room.

"What are you doing home so … oh, Ammi, you don't look well."

"She has a fever. I gave her two Aspirin."

"I'm sorry, Ammi."

"Is everything okay?" her father asks.

"Yes, it's been handled."

"Please stay with mama while I get the bins out."
He exits quickly, as Maya does her best to conceal
her concern … *because the bins are in the shed*.

Madison and Ethan are kneeling on the ground
behind the shed when they hear the back door open,
followed by footsteps. *They freeze*!
Sanjay opens the shed and takes out two garbage
bins. As he walks towards the side walkway, Maya is
at the back door, forcing a smile for her father.

"Is everything alright, dear?"

"Yes, I just needed some air." Sanjay nods and
walks down the walkway. Maya glides over to the
shed to check on her friends, but they've departed.
Maya looks to the sky and smiles, as Sanjay walks up.

"What are you looking at, dear?"

"Just enjoying the beautiful sky." she smiles. As he
and his daughter move towards the back door,
Maya's phone Pings.

"I'll get the door, dear." walking ahead. Maya
takes out her phone. It's a text from Madison. "*Great*
with an airplane emoji and a 'Smiley Face.' Maya
grins, and with another look at the sky, she goes
inside.

13. SO, DAD ...?

Madison and Ethan are serving up dad's favorite blueberry pancakes for breakfast, and wasting no time steering the convo to porting.

"Did watching it make you believe teleporting was possible?" asks Ethan.

"I don't know. I just loved how different the story was."

"Pretty bizarre porting in a car like that." says Madison.

"Totally." says Ethan. "So, Dad, think you'll ever try to go back in time?"

"You mean before you guys were born?"

"Maybe not that far."

"Yeah, like, I don't know, maybe .. 24 hours?" says Madison coyly.

"Why would I want to?"

"Uh, maybe prevent car accidents?" says Ethan.

"That only happens in movies."

"Okay, so someone steals a priceless artwork from a museum in the middle of the night," says Madison, "and there's no clues. Now you port back to last night, hide across the street from the museum and wait for the thief to come. Then you follow him to where he's gone with the artwork and then anonymously call the police and they arrest him."

"You got *all this* from watching Back To The Future?"
Madison looks briefly at her brother.

"Why are you surprised, Dad?" she says. "Out of the millions of people who've watched the film we're the only people who've actually teleported, so it's kind of natural to wonder what if, right?"

"So would you?" asks Ethan.

"Look, you know why I developed the HT, and why I didn't apply for a Patent. So why would I invest more time and energy when Mom and I want to explore the world with you?" he grins.

"Cuz that'd be like the Wright brothers having the only plane in the world and refusing to share their technology." says Ethan.

"Guys, I love your curiosity and passion, but I told you, the world's not ready for the HT. And I have to get to work." He kisses Madison on the cheek, gives Ethan a thumbs up and walks out. Ethan looks at his sister, both very frustrated.

* * *

That evening Madison and Ethan are sitting on their parent's fave two-seater. Hoodies pulled up. Nachos running low. Looking at Madison's phone screen where texts slowly scroll. *very, very cloudy here today .. so depressed,* with several sad face emojis. Maya's reply; *OH, NO*!!! with two shocked face emojis. *Any hope for Sunshine?* Madison's reply; *No. Mr. Sunshine doesn't want to play.* with a sad face emoji crying.

"All her hard work … she's crushed." says Mad'.

"She knew it was a long shot Dad would agree."

"What you said about the Wright brothers was bang on."

"It's true. The HT could save so many lives."

"Yeah." She leans back and closes her eyes. After a moment she sits up, startled. "I just had a horrible thought."

"What?"

"There's people around the world living their lives right now who are going to be robbed or kidnapped this year .. and we could have helped some of them."

"We couldn't save them .. the Police would have to." he grabs a nacho. Madison looks at him.

"Why couldn't we save them?

"You and me? The guy whose never been in a fight snooping on bad guys?" not enthused at all.

"We'd need a policeman." smiling coyly. Ethan's very intrigued now.

"I think he'd be up for it, Mad'."

"Of course he would! … I woke up at three-thirty today … couldn't get back to sleep. So, for five years Dad declined the invitation to go to Mumbai … this year he accepts. Why? Maya reminded him of when he was seventeen at NASA, with no friends. Four months later we went back in time and we watched a car accident that happened eighteen hours earlier."

"I know … it's crazy!" shaking his head.

"And it was *one minute* from never happening!" she says, looking at him closely.

"What do you mean?" brow furrowed.

"Rafael walked out of that cafe right when my bag was stolen … and a month later we're crying with him about Maria."
Ethan chews on that for a moment, then -

"You're right! If he came out a minute later, or a minute earlier, we likely never meet him."

"Yeah … E', we're supposed to be doing this."
He nods his head slightly, and then sighs.

"But that means we'd be lying to Dad and Mom!"

"I know … and it really sucks. But you know they'd never let us do it, right?" she grins.

"Obviously." pulling another nacho. "Have you thought how hard it'd be to keep this a secret?"

"No, I haven't. Look, let's not get ahead of ourselves. Rafael may not be as excited as us. He'll be sleeping now …we'll call him tomorrow after school."
They look at each other …

* * *

14. PLAN 'B'

Rafael was very excited when Madison and Ethan told him on their Zoom the next day that their mom has offered to pay for their flights with her gazillion Air Miles. And this weekend was perfect because he had the weekend off. When they called later to confirm their arrival he was surprised they declined his offer to pick them up at the airport, but secretly pleased when they said they would be arriving at six o'clock in the morning. Of course they couldn't tell him - *not yet* - their 4,750 mile *flight* would arrive whenever they wanted .. and last mere seconds, and the reason for the early arrival was they had to keep it a secret from dad. Rafael suggested *Sergio's*, a popular Cafe on the beach. That suited them just fine because they quickly went online and watched videos of the area nearby. This enabled them to select a secluded place to touch down from their *flight* and they easily acquired their Global Coordinates (GC's).

"It was so good of your parents. Be sure to thank them for me!" as they enjoyed cheese and ham omelettes with rice, a *Sergio* specialty.

"We will." says Madison. "So have you arrested many bad guys?"

"Yes, we captured two Bank robbers last week. My partner, Carlos, he's been on the Force eleven years, so I'm learning from him every day."

"That's great." says Ethan.

"Have you had to use your martial arts?" Madison asks.

"A few times .. guy with a knife, another guy had a baseball bat."

"Sounds pretty scary."

"They're more scared than us because they don't want to be arrested. They panic and make bad decisions. It's part of our training."

"Have you had to use your gun?" asks Ethan.

"No, and I hope I never do."

"It goes with the job, right?" says Madison.

"I've met Officers who've never fired their gun in fifteen years."

"Huh? So what's a typical week for you?"

"I work forty hours. So far it's been two day shifts, one evening shift, then two overnight shifts."

"Must mess up your sleep." says Ethan.

"The overnights, for sure." taking his last bite of omelette. "Delicious."

"Ready to show us the beach?" Madison smiles.

Fifteen minutes later Rafael, Madison and Ethan are sitting in a secluded area two hundred feet from the ocean's surf.

"Ever had a good friend ask if they could tell you something very important but you had to promise you'd never tell anyone?"

"Yeah … I can't remember what … why?" Madison looks briefly at Ethan.

"We need to share something very important with you, but you have to promise us you'll *never, ever* tell anyone."

That quickly crashes the relaxed mood for Rafael. He's concerned. "Is this about your family? Is that why your mama used her …?"

"It's about our family … but we're okay, thanks."

"That's good."

"So, do you promise?" offering her right hand.

"Of course." shaking her hand, then Ethan's.

"How can I help you?"

"First, we need you to know everything we're going to share with you now is the absolute truth. We can provide verifiable proof .. but until you see that proof with your own eyes, you'll think we're totally delulu-crazy."

"Okay …" not sure what to make of this.

Twenty minutes later Rafael is standing ten feet from Madison and Ethan, mouth open, eyebrows raised, looking like he's just seen an alien spaceship. He quickly kneels down and whispers.

"This is absolutely unbelievable, guys! And you had no side effects when you came back?"

"None." Madison says.

"Did it feel weird going back?"

"No. Look, we know you have a million questions like we did." Madison grins as she takes her cast-sleeve from her small backpack and slides it over her left arm. "It looks like a cast for a broken arm, but it's designed to conceal and protect the HT."

"HT?"

"Human Teleport device." says Ethan

"It's inside that?"

"Give me your index finger." Madison says. Rafael extends his right hand and Madison holds his index finger and places it just inside the cast-sleeve near her palm. Rafael's eyes go wide when he sees the small panel slide open, revealing the HT keypad.

"That's the device? It's so small!" looking closely. "It's like a phone! How is it possible?"

"The computers NASA used to get Neil Armstrong on the moon weren't as powerful as the iPhone." says Ethan.

"Really?" He grins. "You're blowing my mind, guys!"

"We know the feeling." grins Madison.

"You ain't seen nothing yet, man." says Ethan.

Twenty minutes later Rafael and Ethan are standing near a huge rock formation looking at Madison as she exhales vigorously. Then she taps the Launch key and … she vanishes in a split second. Rafael is absolutely stunned!

"Where is she, E'?!" aghast, looking in all

directions, as Ethan laughs.

"Arriving in our backyard in a few seconds. I'd get your phone out, man."

Rafael looks at him. *Seriously?* Ethan nods, enjoying this. Rafael gets his phone out just as it rings. He swipes right and sees Madison's smiling face.

"Hey, Rafael, recognize my backyard?" turning her phone around.

Rafael is stunned. "This is like Star Wars, guys!"

"It'll take some time, Rafael." Ethan chuckles as he looks at Madison's face on Rafael's phone screen.

"C'mon back, Mad'."

"Okay, I'll see you in about twenty seconds." she grins, and the screen goes blank.

"Start counting." Ethan grins. Rafael looks at his wristwatch. After several seconds he looks at Ethan, who's grinning. "Couple more seconds." Then -

"Hey, Raf'!" grins Madison, standing behind them. Rafael turns around and throws his arms straight up, eyes wide in disbelief. He rushes to her and puts his hands on her face, then her shoulders to convince himself this is real, as Madison and Ethan laugh loudly

"It's really me, Rafael." He starts to laugh, and then they're hugging each other like little kids.

Ten minutes later Rafael has calmed down a little, sitting on the beach where they were earlier.

"We have to be extremely careful there's no one nearby who could see us launch." says Madison.

"Of course, it would blow their mind. They'd be calling the police." says Rafael.

"They'd think he was hallucinating." Ethan says.

"But we can't take the chance." she says. "So this is where we will meet you before we go on a case. We'll bring your cast-sleeve, and today we'll give you one BNP pill so you'll have it when we go on our first case."

"I take it without water thirty minutes before we teleport, right?"

"Yes, so as soon as we know we're porting, take it." says Ethan.

"When we return after we've finished the case, we'll have another pill for you for our next case." says Madison.

"Where should I keep my sleeve?"

"We'll take it with us. Dad only made a few backups, so if he sees there's one missing we've got a problem." says Ethan.

"Good. So what type of crimes will we be investigating?"

"We'll start with small crimes to get comfortable doing it." says Ethan.

"That's smart. And they have to be in the past twenty-four hours?"

"Yes. Maya will be checking, and we'll look for small crimes in the US."

"I can check locally. There's a lot of burglaries in Palma. Okay, so we got back in time when we know the robbery took place. I obviously can't arrest them, so, what's the plan?"

"We'll get video of the criminals with our video glasses…" she begins.

"Wait! Video glasses?"

"Have you seen the glasses with a small square on top of the frame near the lens?" Ethan asks.

"No"

"I was able to hide the technology inside the frame." He puts on his video glasses. "Whatever we see will be recorded, and when we're back in present time Maya will download it to her computers so she can see what we saw." says Ethan.

"When we go back in time she can't see it because we're in an alternate realm." adds Madison.

"This is unbelievable! Every Police Force should have this, Ethan."

"I'm still perfecting it, so there's no Patent."

"Tell him about the tracking devices."

"You guys have tracking devices, too?"

"Yeah, and my Drone Bird delivers them." Ethan shows him DB. "Me and my best friend, Garret, developed it. It can fly up to a hundred yards, controlled by my HT keypad. Garrett doesn't know this, but I can put a tiny tracking chip inside a small amount of white stuff I make that looks exactly like bird poop. I'll show you." Rafael is mesmerized.

He takes out a small zip-lock bag and removes a small substance that he places on DB's feet. "It's kinda like plasticine." Ethan taps a few numbers on his keypad and DB flies over to a big rock one hundred feet away.

"I tap another key .. and watch." DB drops the substance on the rock. They run to the rock to take a look.

"We did a test for Maya and she was able to track the truck DB pooped on."

"That's fantastic, Ethan!" grins Rafael.

"There's more." says Madison. "Maya can hack into the CCTV of every city in the world. If the PTC is on the vehicle, she can track it in present time, or re-wind the CCTV."

"This is amazing! How is it that Maya has all this technology to get intel!"

"Intel … love it!" grins Ethan.

"We can't tell you, Rafael. Let's just say she's incredibly talented and important people know it."

"Okay …" says Rafael, clearly mind-blown now.

"We live in three Time Zones, which will be a challenge." says Madison. "If Maya learns of a case in the morning that happened 15 hours ago we only have a nine hour window to go back. But nine in the morning in Mumbai is ten-thirty in the evening for E' and me, and three in the morning for you." Rafael nods. "Or I'm working, and you're in classes?"

"Right. So we'll only take a case if we can all go. If you're on a shift, we won't go."

"I'd never let you guys go alone."

"Thanks, Rafael." Madison says.

"Do I need to bring my gun?"

"Oh, gosh no! We're only witnessing the crime." she says.

"Good, because if I had to shoot someone to protect you guys, the ballistics report would trace the bullet back to my gun."

"No guns, and hopefully no fighting." says Madison.

"Sure hope not, I've never been in one."

"I'll teach you how to take care of yourself."

"Okay, cool." grins Ethan.

"Oh, and my friends call me Raf." he says.

"Okay, Raf." Madison smiles.

"Mad', Maya, Raf and E'. … we're a team." grins Ethan.

"Let's give Maya the great news." says Madison.

***

Maya and Meta are enjoying their ice cream following her morning therapy at the Rehab.

"Have you spoken with Madison and Ethan this week?"

"Yes, this was Madison's last week at camp. Classes begin next week. And Ethan is doing well with his lawn care business."

"The Giller's are such good people. It's too bad they're so far away."

"Yes, but we have Zooms, which is nice." Maya's phone pings.

"Young people today are so lucky with all this

technology."

Maya opens her phone and looks at the screen. A 'selfie' of Madison, Ethan and Rafael, smiling, thumbs up. The text reads; *What a Team*!!!! Maya chokes back a gasp.

"Is everything alright, Maya?"

"Yes, Ammi, it is very good news from work." smiling.

"It's not for me to know. I'm just glad it makes you happy." Meta smiles.

Maya can barely contain her excitement.

* * *

15. READY TO GO!

Madison is catching up with Rebecca and Natalie at lunch on their first day back to school after Summer break.

"We went to Rome for a week and did the wine valley tours."

"Did your parents let you drink?" asks Natalie.

"A few times. Did you know kids as young as twelve there drink wine?"

"Seriously?" says Madison

"Oh, yeah, the locals thought my dad was delulu not letting me drink." sips her soda.

"How was your Summer, Mad'? Anything new or exciting happen?"

"Good. Camp was a lot of fun with the kids. Took some trips with mom and dad an' E'."

"Cool. Where'd you go?" says Rebecca.

Mumbai five times. Majorca four times, day trips to Buenos Aires and Rio...

"My uncle's cottage, and we went to Frisco for a weekend. How was the cottage, Nat'?" shifting the focus away from herself.

"First ten days were gucci. Worked on my tan, tried waterskiing - it's so hard! Then it rained for three days, so I streamed, an' read a good book."

"Romance or mystery?" Rebecca asks.

"Skin and hair care."

Rebecca and Madison chuckle. "That's not a *book*, Nat'!" says Rebecca.

"Yeah, well my skin and hair have never looked better, don't you think?" primping.

* * *

Coach Jamieson is speaking with the girls after the *Rebels* first practice.

"Looks like you didn't hit the gym in Europe, Rebecca." Her teammates razz her.

"Too much vino, Bec'!" draws more chuckles.

"First exhibition match is a week Friday, so I need you to get your minds focused so we're ready to go. It's a long season and we want to get off to a fast start like last season." Coach walks away, and Madison and Natalie grin at Rebecca.

"How'd she know you were in Europe?" Natalie asks.

"She asked me how my Summer was, what was I supposed to say?"

"Hope no one tells her about Jason's party on Saturday. She'll likely put us on curfew." says Rebecca.

"Too bad I'm gonna miss it." Madison says, looking disappointed.

"Why?" asks Rebecca.

"Goin' to Palo Alto to meet a Professor."

"You'll be jet-laggin' at practice Monday." says Natalie. Madison shrugs.

Madison had lost count of how many *little white lies* she'd told since her and Ethan's life had changed forever after meeting Maya. It wasn't like she was keeping a Little White Lies Notebook, of course, because it would be really dangerous having a written summary of why she'd had to tell a *LWL*, along with details of where they had gone and what they did. In the past few months Maya had refused to do any Zoom Calls with them because of the risk of leaving what she called 'fingerprints' that could be traced to conversations, texts or e-mails that a hacker could access. But now that they were going forward with their plan to bring criminals to justice, Maya knew they would have to be able to communicate without so many restrictions. Madison and Ethan have ported to Mumbai for a meeting with Maya while her parents are out for dinner..

"I may get a great lead on a case at eleven in the evening here and I've got to be able to speak with you guys and Raf so we can make a fast decision if we're going to take on a case."

"But you said Zooms and phone calls are too dangerous." says Madison.

"They are if you don't have your own dedicated server that no one knows about, and even if they did find it, it's got alarm systems in place to alert me."

"How do you get a dedicated server?" Madison

asks.

"I'm guessing she's already got one." Ethan grins, and Maya smiles.

"I do. You guys and Raf need to get cheap burner phones so there's no record of you owning them. This will allow us to do Zoom calls to discuss very sensitive details about cases. When the Zoom ends I'll erase all your data so if someone steals your phone there's no data on it."

"This is great, Maya." says Madison.

"There's another problem we'll have to deal with eventually." says Ethan. "We'll be using a lot of Body Neutralizing Pills, and Dad's going to notice."

"And it's expensive to make." adds Madison.

"He won't give you the formula?" Madison and Ethan shake their heads. Maya bites her lip, thinking. "There's only one solution … but it's your decision." It only takes a few seconds for Madison to realize what the 'decision' is.

"You want to hack into Dad's computer?"

"Unless you have a better idea." Maya shrugs. Madison looks at Ethan. *Oh, man!*

Thirty minutes later Maya is removing a new USB external drive with a very precious File inside, which she immediately secures in a small box hidden inside a wall behind her desk.

"You'll never have the ingredients written down." Maya says. "When you go to buy them, you'll call me and I'll tell you what you need, and how much to buy. Looks like you'll need part-time jobs, and I can help out, too, of course."

"I've got fourteen hundred saved up from cutting grass. And it's pretty much year round."

"I saved over a thousand from my Camp job."

"Good. Okay, I need Rafael's work schedule each week so I know when he's definitely not available … your class times … and *Rebels* games."

"I'll have it for you every Sunday evening." says Madison.

"Excellent. Okay, you should get going in case my parents come home early again." They laugh.

* * *

16. FIRST CASE!

Madison, Ethan and Rafael were itching to go on their first case. Each day Maya was checking online every few hours to see if a break and enter robbery of a store or home had occurred where the Police had few good leads. Those types of crimes rarely made the news, so Maya started hacking into local Police Stations in multiple cities looking for crime leads that fit the bill. Madison and Ethan had started watching the local news every morning at breakfast to see if their News Anchor, Lyla Wiggons, was reporting similar crimes where they would have enough time to teleport back to witness when the crime took place. Madison, Ethan and dad are eating breakfast, watching the News.

"I'm impressed you're taking an interest in world news." says dad.
Ethan, sipping his blueberry smoothie, sneaks a quick look at his sister.

"The political talking heads bore me." says Ethan. "But sometimes they have good features on people doing good things around the country."

"Like the one about the homeless mother and her son." says Madison.

"Yes, and the person who donated five thousand dollars and didn't want to give his name." says dad. "That's inspiring, and it has a ripple effect because maybe a million people saw that story and it got them thinking they could do something to help someone less fortunate. It could be deciding to give a homeless person five bucks instead of a dollar." He takes the last gulp of caffeine.

"Okay guys, have a great day." He stands and kisses Madison on the cheek and fist bumps Ethan.

"You, too, Dad." says Madison.

Madison and Ethan were going to classes with two cell phones now. Their regular one, and their new burner phones they paid cash for at Walmart that are set to vibrate for calls or texts from Maya. The first four days their burner buzzed twice a day, but Maya was only calling to report she hadn't found a case yet, and to see if they'd had any luck. So when Madison's burner buzzes after dinner on the fifth day she figures it's likely nothing, as she walks out onto the deck.

"Hey Maya."

"I found a perfect case for us." she says excitedly.

"Really!? Hold on … E'" she calls out. Ethan comes out and when he sees Madison's smile and thumbs up, he rushes over and leans close to her so he can hear the convo - *on speaker is too risky.*

"A man in New Orleans lost his job two months ago and his truck insurance lapsed so he wasn't driving it. It was stolen from his garage today. He's married with four young kids."

"What's our window?" asks Madison.

"Nine hours."

"Is Raf' available?" Ethan asks.

"Yes."

"It's nine o'clock. We"ll have to wait two hours 'till dad goes to bed." Madison says.

"Tell Raf' we'll pick him up, when E?" looking at him. "Just after five in the morning." he says. "And remind him to take his BNP pill now."

Two hours later Rafael is on the beach in Majorca, clad all in black, waiting for Madison and Ethan's arrival.

"Hey, Raf'." says Madison walking up behind him with Ethan, both in black.

"Hey, guys." he smiles, and they hug. Madison puts her DAC in her right ear. Ethan hands a DAC to Rafael. "Can you hear me, Maya?"

"Copy."

"Guys, this is the first of what we hope will be many cases helping people. Before we launch, I want to say a few words." Madison holds her hands out and they clasp hands. She lowers her head, Ethan and Rafael do, too. "Father, we know Maria is safe and at peace with you now, and we ask that you keep us safe tonight. Maria, you inspired us to help others who have suffered injustice. We never met you, but we'll never forget you and you will always be in our hearts. For as long as we are together to bring bad people to justice, we'll dedicate each case to your beautiful memory. Amen"

"That was beautiful, thanks, Mad'."

"You ready, guys?" they nod their heads.

"We're goin' dark, Maya." says Ethan.

Clive Borges has not had an easy life. His parents divorced when he was four years old and he was raised by his mother and her parents. School was a challenge and he dropped out his Junior year to take a course to become an electrician. He got a job, met a woman and five years later they had four ankle biters, as the Aussies like to say. Clive has never been able to cobble together enough cash to make a down payment on anything more expensive than the 2011 Ford Explorer he bank-financed five years ago. He's made every payment, and last month when the options were pay his vehicle insurance or the bank, the bank won in a unanimous decision. Clive's been taking the bus to job interviews the past few weeks, praying for a break. Instead, he got a break-in when persons unknown hot-wired his Ford Explorer parked in front of his rented apartment in the four-plex. The engine's roar woke up Clive from a fitful sleep at twenty-five minutes after three o'clock yesterday morning, but when he dashed outside, the truck was gone. He called the Police and they dispatched a black and white to investigate, but they basically told Clive he'd seen his Ford Explorer for the last time. No job. No truck. No insurance. Bank owed about eleven grand. It's not a stretch to say Clive needs a miracle. As he lay in bed this evening, worrying himself sick, he had no way of knowing four teenagers from three countries were trying to help him.

Madison, Ethan and Rafael have just arrived from Majorca and are kneeling behind a thick hedge across the street and five doors down from Clive's apartment, where his 2011 Ford Explorer is parked.

"My heart's beating about a hundred an' eighty." whispers Ethan.

"Take a deep breath, hold it for seven seconds, and exhale." Raf says. Ethan does as instructed. "Keep doing that as you get DB ready. We need PTC's (*Poop Tracker Chip*) on the Explorer and the bad guy's vehicle."

Ethan attaches the PTC to DB's feet. Seconds later they are alerted by the sound of a black SUV approaching. Then the headlights are turned off.

"This must be the robbers." whispers Rafael. The SUV stops and the engine is cut. The driver and front passenger doors open and are closed without a sound by two men all in black, wearing ball caps. They look around to make sure no insomniacs are looking out windows. They get to the Explorer and one of the men slides a long piece of metal between the door and the window. Both men are so focused on the task they don't notice DB flying over their

SUV and depositing a PTC onto the roof.

"Good job. Wait for my signal." Rafael barely whispers, as they watch the carjackers gain entry to Clive's Explorer. The driver door closes, and the second guy runs back to his SUV. He turns on the ignition and drives up just past the Explorer.

Rafael nods to Ethan, his signal to send DB. Ethan taps a few keys on his HT device and DB flies across the street, twenty feet above the Explorer just as its engine roars to life. DB hovers overhead, out of the driver's vision, and a PTC lands on the roof. As the two vehicles race off into the night, Clive comes running out in his underwear. Seeing his uninsured vehicle disappear he unleashes a guttural scream that would have broken his mama's heart if she was alive.

Five minutes later Madison, Ethan and Rafael are in New Orleans in present time (PT) speaking with Maya via their DAC's.

"I've got CCTV coverage for New Orleans traffic zones on the route they're taking. They've driven three miles and stopped twice for traffic lights. So, was it exciting?"

"I was really nervous, Maya." Ethan says.

"He did an awesome job." says Rafael.

"Let's hope they didn't drive too far." says Madison.

"In my training I learned car thieves get off the road as quickly as possible in case they get pulled over by Police."

"When they do, what's the plan, Maya?" Madison asks.

"I'll get your GC's to port there because we have to confirm the Explorer is still there. It may not be … it's been over twenty-one hours."

"How will you contact the Police?" Ethan asks.

"I have an encrypted phone line they can't trace, and I'll use an AI-generated voice to speak with a male, New Orleans accent."

"Very cool."

"They're stopping again … hope it's not another traffic light."

There's four-squares on one of Maya's monitors showing four traffic zones.

"I'm checking the location, guys." Twenty seconds later, "They stopped at an industrial park." looking at a photo on her other monitor. "I'll have your GC's in a few seconds."

Ninety seconds later Madison, Ethan and Rafael are on the roof of the industrial park where Maya tracked Clive's stolen Explorer last night.

"There's no one here and no security, Maya." says Ethan. "And there's a lot of windows. Maybe DB can get some good video for you."

He releases DB to fly down a few feet and hover, the camera in its mouth recording what he can see. Because they are in **PT** (*Present Time*) Maya has linked her monitors to DB's camera, so she's seeing in real time what DB is recording.

"The Explorer is there, guys!"

"Fantastic!" says Madison.

"That's great!" Rafael says.

"Can you tip-off the police now?" asks Ethan.

"I sure can."

Madison, Ethan and Rafael hug and hi-5 excitedly.

"What a great feeling!" says Madison. "Wish you were here, Maya. You made all this happen."

"Thanks, we're a great team, guys."

* * *

Two mornings later Madison and Ethan are having breakfast with Dr. G, watching the Morning News with Lyla Wiggons.

"We have a really nice story for you from our New Orleans affiliate."

Madison looks at Ethan, as a female reporter appears on the screen.

"I'm with Clive Borges, an electrician in New Orleans and the father of four children. Mr. Borges recently lost his job and couldn't afford to pay the insurance on his truck. Just after three o'clock on Tuesday morning he was awakened by thieves stealing his uninsured Ford Explorer. Mr. Borges, can you tell our viewers how this affected you?

Clive looks shyly into the camera. He's a skinny man, late 30's.

"That's right, ma'am, I got laid off an' couldn't make the insurance payment on the truck. I owe the bank eleven thousand, so I was at the end of my rope. So me an' Betsy, my wife, we got down on our knees and we prayed to God that He would deliver us a miracle. And did He ever. I can't explain it, but some Good Samaritan found where my truck had been taken. The Lord works in mysterious ways, you know, and by golly, the Officer came by yesterday and said they'd found my truck. Betsy an' me just cried our eyes out, thanking Jesus for delivering us from our troubles."

"Isn't that great." says Dr. G., looking at Madison and Ethan.

"Amazing." says Ethan, as Madison gets up quickly and rushes out. Ethan follows.

He walks down the hallway and taps softly on the bathroom door. It opens, and Madison is crying happy tears. She pulls him inside, closes the door and hugs him.

"I'm so happy for them .. we did that E'." she sniffs. "This feels better than any goal I ever scored."

"Yeah, it feels awesome."

"We're gonna help so many people, E'."
There's a soft knock on the door.

"You okay, Mad'?" says dad softly. Ethan opens the door.

"Yeah … that story got to her."

"I wish there were more like that." dad says, opening his arms for her. They hug.

"Thanks, Dad."

"Have a good day. See you tonight." and he walks

away.

As soon as Dr. G left, Madison texted Maya and Rafael the link to the interview with Clive. It was six-thirty in the evening in Mumbai, and two-thirty in the afternoon in Majorca. Minutes later the four teens are on a Zoom.

"What an amazing feeling seeing Clive so happy!" says Raphael.

"I burst into tears, I was so happy." says Maya, sniffling.

"Mad' said it felt better than any goal she's scored."

"We're gonna help so many people, I can feel it." Maya says.

"There's a lot of Clive's out there, we just have to find them." says Madison.

"We will." says Rafael.

"I know we will." says Maya.

* * *

17. PAY IT FORWARD

After the *Rebels* practice that afternoon the players are doing the dreaded sprints - from the goal to mid-field and back to the goal two times. Madison is going all-out, as always, setting the standard for her teammates to follow. She's also getting updates from Maya on her search for their 'next Clive', via the DAC in her right ear.

"Raf' says there's no cases in Majorca that are inside our window. I've been checking small towns in the US and Europe, but most of the one's I find are past twenty-four hours."
Madison has finished her sprints, leaning over, hands on her knees.

"Okay, we'll be online tonight." she whispers.

"Talking to yourself, Mad'? grins Rebecca, as Madison looks up.

"Yeah, just saying how much I hate doing these."

"And again!" shouts Coach Jamieson, which is met with a chorus of groans. Madison leads the way.

"I really hate doing sprints after practice, Maya." she whispers.

"Don't hate them, Mad'. You're very fortunate you can do them."

"Oh, gosh, I'm so sorry, Maya. That was so bad of me!"

"It's okay."
Madison picks up the pace. Now she's running like she's being chased by a hungry, angry bear.

Coach Jamieson takes note as she watches Madison make the turn at mid-field and continue her blistering pace towards the goal.

"That's what makes you special, Mad'." Coach says softly, smiling.

* * *

Madison's enjoying a salmon filet right off the barbecue tonight, and Ethan and Dad are chowing down on steaks on the back deck.

"Decided where you'd like to go next?"

"I think we should wait a few weeks, Dad."
Madison says. "I'm running out of excuses for Bec' and Nat'."

"Ditto with Garrett."

"You and mom should go." says Madison.

"Yeah, go snorkelling in Rio or Majorca."

"Maybe we'll do Majorca in the morning and Rio in the afternoon!" Dad grins.

* * *

It's eight-thirty on Saturday morning and Dr. G is carefully closing the back door as quietly as possible so he won't wake up his kids. He's porting to Rio de Janeiro to meet Mrs. G for a leisurely day of snorkelling, good food and sandy beaches. What he doesn't know is Madison and Ethan are awake and peeking out their bedroom windows because they have big plans of their own today.

Ten hours ago Rafael texted Madison while working a midnight shift with his partner, Carlos. They were the first police to arrive at the scene of a robbery at the home of an eighty-four year old widow. Rafael managed to sneak off for a quick chat with Madison and Ethan.

"Mrs. Gonzalez recently learned of several eye doctors who perform operations at no charge to restore the vision of people in Africa. They're raising funds to purchase more equipment. Mrs. Gonzalez was donating a diamond necklace worth a hundred thousand dollars to an auction raising funds for the doctors. She's very upset."

"Wasn't it insured?" asks Madison.

"It was, but it will take time to process her claim and the doctors are counting on her funds by next week to purchase the equipment."

They decided the recovery of Mrs. Gonzalez's diamond necklace will be their second case. Rafael's shift would be over in four hours, which is two in the morning in Merritt Island. He needed to get some sleep, but they'd still have lots of hours left on their 24-hour window to teleport back to witness the robbery.

* * *

It's three o'clock on a sunny, Saturday afternoon in Majorca. Madison and Ethan have arrived on the beach at their usual rendezvous place behind the rocks. Rafael is fresh from six hour sleep and he's very motivated to put a smile on Mrs. Gonzalez's face. They're speaking with Maya on their DAC's, where it's one-thirty Sunday morning in Mumbai.

"I downloaded your GC's to Mrs. Gonzalez's street. Raf' said there's lots of big bushes and trees to hide behind."

"Okay guys, let's find Mrs. Gonzalez's diamond necklace." says Raf'.

One minute later Madison, Ethan and Rafael have ported back almost twelve hours and are kneeling behind thick bushes four houses down from Mrs. Gonzalez's home. Video glasses on.

"How would the robbers know she had a valuable necklace?" Ethan asks.

"I don't know. Maybe someone from the auction house tipped them off."

"She's very wealthy, huh?" Ethan says.

"Her husband died four years ago. They didn't have children, and after she heard about the eye doctors she decided she wanted to help people now, not after she dies."

"That's really good of her." Madison says.

"She's a wonderful lady," Raf says.

Ten minutes later a dark, two-door sedan slows down and the headlights are turned off before it parks right in front of the bushes where the teens are hiding! They remain still, not even whispering, until the man, late 30's, in black jeans and shirt, has walked four doors down and goes up the front steps to Mrs. Gonzalez's home.

"E', put a PTC on the rear fender as well." says Raf'. Ethan gets DB loaded up and he taps a few keys on his HT keypad. DB flies off twenty feet and drops a PTC on the back fender of the thief's sedan. Then DB flies back and Ethan loads him up again. DB flies back and drops a PTC on the roof near the passenger side.

"Mrs. Gonzalez woke up while he was in the house. She was terrified."

"She must have been terrified." Madison says. A few minutes later the thief is running from the house as a light is turned on in the second floor. The teens remain very still as the thief quickly gets in his sedan and it accelerates down the street.

"Let's get back to PT (Present Time), guys." says Rafael.

Ninety seconds later one of Maya's monitors is playing recorded CCTV video of the street the thief drove on after the robbery, thanks to DB's PTC. The sedan drives past one of the CCTV cameras.

"I'm tracking him. He's gone three miles, observing the speed limit."

"We'll wait here." says Raf, with Madison and Ethan behind the big rocks on the Majorca beach where many are enjoying the late afternoon sun.

"Did your parents teleport today?"

"Yeah, Rio. They just discovered snorkelling." Madison says.

"I love to snorkel. You guys?"

"We've gone twice. Here and Rio." says Ethan.

"One day I'll take you to a great spot to turtle dive."

"Cool." says Ethan.

"That'd be great." Madison says.

"Guys, he stopped for over two minutes. That's too long for a red light, so I Google Earth'd the area and there's a jewelry store right there. Adriano Joyeria."

"Maybe that's his buyer." Raf says.

"Adriano will have security video inside and outside. I need to access it."

"How do you do that?" Ethan asks.

"I'll tell you after I do it. I'll need about thirty minutes. Grab a cold drink."

"Copy that, Maya." Raf' says.

Madison and Ethan put on their ball caps and shades and walked with Rafael to get a cold drink, then sat down on the beach to wait for good news.

"If someone from the auction house tipped off the thief, how long would they go to prison for?" Ethan asks.

"Depends if they have previous convictions. If they don't, they could make a deal with the Prosecutor to testify against the thief."

"They don't care all those people in Africa won't get the help they need." says Madison.

"Yeah, there's a lot of bad people." Rafael says.

"And we're gonna put a lot of them in prison." grins Ethan.

Maya Google'd Adriano Joyeria to get their website address. Then she did a 'Whois' search for their domain registration which gave her their e-mail address and internet provider. She hacked into the IP accounts department to find Adriano's, which revealed who they bank with. She hacked into the bank's server, located Adriano's account and checked their last month's debits to see if there's one for a security company. There it was. *Palma Seguridad.* She hacked into their server and in minutes she had accessed Adriano's security hard drive inside the store. She's looking at one of her monitors where security video is playing from inside Adriano's store.

"I'm in, guys. I'll know soon if Mrs. Gonzalez's necklace is here."

"You're unbelievable, Maya!" says Madison, via her DAC.

"He stopped his car at four twenty-five …"

looking closely at the top right corner of the monitor where the digital time-code begins to move rapidly. But in seconds Maya taps a key to stop the video because the man who stole Mrs. Gonzalez's necklace has just entered from the rear of the store!

"Guys, a man matching your description of the thief entered the jewelry store just before four-thirty this morning!" looking at the video time code stopped at 04:26:44.

"Amazing, Maya!" says Raf'.

"He's walking into an office …" where another security camera records him kneeling down at a wall safe. He reads from a scrap of paper as he enters the Code. He opens the door, places the diamond necklace inside, then closes the door as the video stops. Maya notes the time code: 04:29:04 and writes the numbers on a pad.

"Guys, he put Mrs. Gonzalez's necklace in a wall safe at twenty-nine minutes after four!"

"Can you call the Police now?" Ethan asks.

"No, I need to see if anyone removed it in the past thirteen hours … which I'll know in a minute." She taps a key and the video resumes playing, now fast-forwarding. Maya watches closely, not blinking, and after about a minute she stops the video and makes note of the time code: 19:21:45.

"Guys, Mrs. Gonzalez's necklace has been in a wall safe at Adriano's since four-thirty this morning."

On the Majorca beach the teens are ecstatic.

"That's fantastic!!" says Rafael, standing up with

Madison and Ethan. As they run along the beach -

"You're amazing, Maya!" says Madison.

"Call the number I gave you." says Raf excitedly, "tell them you know where the necklace is."

"Copy that! I'll use an AI-generated Spanish woman's voice who sounds like she's not happy."

"I love it, Maya!" grins Madison, as the teens get behind the big rocks and Rafael pulls off his cast-sleeve and gives it to Madison.

"I hope headquarters calls me and Carlos to return the necklace to Mrs. Gonzalez. I'll call you later." The teens hug.

"Thanks, Raf'!" says Madison.

"We're two-for-two!" grins Ethan.

"Maya, don't forget to scrub our VG video." says Madison. "If Dad ever saw that he'd ground us forever."

* * *

An hour later Rafael and Carlos are sitting with Mrs. Gonzalez in her living room. She's holding the necklace.

"How did you find it so fast?"
Rafael shrugs and looks at Carlos.

"Good Police work, Mrs. Gonzalez."

"I never thought I'd see it again. My Prayers were answered.

"All those people in Africa will have better vision now because of your kindness, Mrs. Gonzalez."

says Rafael.

"It fills my heart with joy thinking of them. I was not able to have children, so this is a way for me to show my gratitude for the good life I had with my husband. Thank you for letting me hold it one more time, Officers." She stands and shakes hands with them.

***

The next morning Madison is pouring a smoothie for Ethan as dad walks in.

"Hey, Dad, how was Rio?" Madison smiles.

"Great! We snorkelled .. had a delicious lunch .. snorkelled again .. had a siesta under a tree on the beach .. then we found a great restaurant for dinner."

"Glad you had a great day."

"Mom said it could only have been better if you guys were with us."

"We'll go next time." says Ethan.

"What'd you guys do?"
Madison looks at Ethan for a nano second. *E' and I went to Majorca to help Raf' track a thief who stole a diamond necklace.*

"Just took it easy." Madison shrugs.

"Yeah, it was nice just chilling." says Ethan, adding banana slices to his toast with **PB**.

"We're thinking of Sosua in the Dominican Republic next Saturday. The guide told us they have great beaches and great snorkelling."

"You guys are really into it." Ethan says.

"Yeah, big time. Give it some thought."

"We will." Madison says.

* * *

The week flew by quickly. When they were not in classes, Madison and Ethan scoured online for 'Breaking News' of robberies. Maya and Rafael were doing the same because the feelings they experienced after helping Clive and Mrs. Gonzalez were so exhilarating. There was no guarantee they'd find a case, of course, and Madison and Ethan knew it would seem odd to mom and dad if they suddenly showed less interest in porting. So they did their pre-trip research on Sosua before their Saturday trip, which they're telling dad at breakfast on Friday.

"Sosua has a very interesting history" says Madison. "It was founded by Jews escaping from Nazi Germany from 1940 to 1945."

"Really?" he says, eating cereal.

"The Dominican government gave visas and land to eight hundred German and Austrian Jews."

"Why'd they do that?"

"There was an agreement with Jewish businessmen from New York." Ethan says.

"Huh? Is Sosua as big as Palma?"

"No, just under fifty thousand." Madison says.

"Can't wait to see it."

"It's the same time-zone, so we don't have to get up early." says Ethan.

"That's good. Okay, have a great day, guys."

Rafael was really enjoying his new career. His partner Carlos is an eleven year veteran with Palma Police and every day he's sharing his experience with his protégé.

"After my fourth year they promoted me to the undercover team."

"That sounds exciting."

"Yeah, it's all single men and women because the hours are crazy. Some cases I was away from home for two to four weeks."

"What kind of cases?"

"Drugs. Illegal guns. Extortion. They gave me an alias with a criminal record in Australia. I'd get intel from an informant and gain the trust of members in these gangs."

"Why was your record in Australia?"

"It reduced the chance they knew a prisoner I should have known. You know, 'Hey, was Sergio Bautista there during your stretch?' If I say, 'Yeah, I knew him', but they just made it up to test me, I'd get a bullet in the head."

"Whoa! You had to be able to think very fast."

"You have no idea. The key is *never* let them see you unnerved because that will betray you every time. My heart would be beating two hundred but you look at me and I was totally calm. If they asked me a question I didn't have an answer for I'd take a long pull on my beer to give me an extra five seconds to think, or I'd say 'Why do you wanna know?' or 'I don't have to tell you that!' and just stare them down. Always show strength, Rafael, never fear."

"Good advice. How long were you undercover?"

"Just over three years. That's the burnout rate. I met Estella in my third year and I knew she was the one, so I asked to be transferred. Palma's five hundred miles away from that life, it's all behind me now."

"Do you ever worry they'll find you?"

"Let's just say I'm extra cautious. And you'll never see my photo in a newspaper after a big arrest."

"Does Estella know you were undercover?"

"Oh, yeah, but I made it sound like it wasn't that dangerous, you know?"

"Sure."

"I don't want her sleeping with one eye open."

"If they offered it to me … undercover, would you recommend I do it?"

"You gotta do what's right for you. When they offered it I had no ties. And it sounded very exciting."

"Yeah, it does. Would they hold it against me if I turned it down?"

"No, it's your life, Raf', it's your decision. You have a girlfriend?"

"No. Some day I want to have what you have. I love kids."

"Yeah, I love my life." smiles Carlos.

18. SAVING SARAH

The Giller's arrived in Sosua just after nine o'clock on Saturday morning. Dr. G had scoured online for snorkelling tours and booked one starting in an hour that included lunch. They're on a much smaller boat than the luxury catamaran in Rio, but the crystal clear, green waters of the Atlantic Ocean are just as impressive. Madison and Ethan explored the marine life with their parents, along with their two guides and other guests. Then they enjoyed a delicious buffet lunch.

When mom and dad ported to Rio de Janeiro last weekend they took their DAC's with them in case they needed to contact Madison and Ethan. But when they travel together like today, they don't need them. So they're unaware that Madison and Ethan brought their DAC's, and are listening right now to Maya.

"Sorry to interrupt your day, guys, but you're going to want to hear this."

"E', let's catch some D."

"Put more sunscreen on." says mom, as her kids walk twenty-five feet away.

"Okay, Maya" says Madison softly.

"Ten hours ago an eleven year old girl in New Jersey was kidnapped from her bed."

"That's terrible!" Madison says softly, thinking of Maria. "Do they have any leads?"

"Her parents were awakened by their dog barking and saw she wasn't in her bed."

"Is Raf' working?"

"His shift ends in an hour."

"We have to rescue her. What's her name?"

"Sarah. When will you be home?"

"It'll be late, Dad's made dinner reservations." says Ethan.

"We have to get home now, E!" whispers Madison urgently.

"Mad's right. Every minute is crucial in cases like this."

"I'll think of something, Maya. Tell Raf to be ready."

Ten minutes later Madison is giving a performance that would impress Margot Robbie.

"I don't feel good, mom. I have chills. It just came over me."

"Oh, no. I wonder if it's something you ate today?"

"No, it would take longer to notice." says dad.

"Yeah, I had the same as Mad', and I'm fine. If you wanna go home, I'll go with you." Ethan kindly offers, performing his role well.

"I hate to ruin your day."

"It's okay, not like we saved up for two years to come here."

"That's very good of you, E." says mom. The boat was moored for lunch six hundred meters from shore, so it was a quick hop aboard the twelve footer the Tour operator had for emergencies like this. Ethan assisted Madison out of the boat and onto the beach.

"They may be watching, so walk slowly." advises Ethan smartly, his arm around her for support. Once they are behind the restaurant and out of view of their concerned parents, they run like they're being chased by a cheetah on that African trip that's on their list of places to port to.

"Very impressive, guys." says Maya.

"Tell Raf' we'll meet him in ten minutes." Madison says.

"Copy that."

Two minutes later Madison and Ethan are running into 16 Fairfield for a quick change of clothes. Minutes later they're on the Majorca beach giving Rafael his cast-sleeve. He pulls it over his muscular left arm as they're speaking with Maya via their DAC's.

"I downloaded your GC's and set your port to arrive fifteen minutes before the dog's barking woke Sarah's parents."

"Copy that." says Rafael. "What are the stake-out ops?"

"I Google-Earth'd the street. Not many trees or hedges. Should be vehicles in driveways close by."

"Copy that."

Fifteen minutes later Madison, Ethan and Rafael have been in Essex County, New Jersey for thirteen minutes. They're across the street from Sarah's upscale home, kneeling behind a Range Rover. Video glasses on.

"Should be anytime now, guys." whispers Raf, his hoodie tight to his face.

"What kind of person abducts an eleven year old girl?" says Ethan.

"Someone looking to make a lot of money." says Raf. "These people are very wealthy."

"Here comes a car." whispers Ethan. looking down the road. The headlights of the four-door car are turned off as it reverses into a driveway and stops. The driver and female passenger look out the windows in all directions. They pull dark hoodies over their heads, obscuring their faces and slowly open their doors and get out. They silently close the doors and then jog around to the back of the house.

"That woman means it's a ransom." says Raf.

"Why?" asks Ethan.

"If he was a sicko he'd be alone. So time's on our side."

"Good." says Madison.

"When we hear the dog barking they'll be coming out with Sarah." says Raf, looking at Ethan loading a

PTC onto DB's feet. "We need a close look at the licence tag, too."

Ethan taps a few keys on his HT keypad and DB flies off. It hovers low in front of the sedan's licence tag, then moves up and drops the PTC onto the hood. DB flies back to Ethan to get loaded up for Round two. DB flies over to the car and drops a PTC on the space between the front grill and fender and flies back to Ethan.

It's not long before they hear the dog barking loudly, and the kidnappers are running down the drive towards their vehicle. The man is carrying a limp Sarah as lights come on in an upstairs room. He climbs in the rear seat with Sarah, as the woman gets in the driver's seat. The engine roars to life and the car accelerates rapidly down the street, lights out. Seconds later Sarah's anguished mother and father rush out. Watching the car speed away, she sobs loudly and falls into his arms.

"Those poor parents." whispers Madison.

"Let's get back and see if our VG vid helps Maya." says Raf, as Madison is watching the parents rush back to their home.

"We're going to get your daughter back" she says softly.

It's two-thirty on Sunday morning in Mumbai and Maya is looking at one of her monitors reviewing the video from Madison, Ethan and Rafael's video glasses, and DB's video. They have returned to PT in

New Jersey, miles away from Sarah's home which they know will now be surrounded by Police and FBI agents investigating her kidnapping. Maya completes her review very efficiently. "I hacked into the State motor vehicle database and ran the licence tag. The car is registered to a seventy-seven year old woman, so it was obviously stolen."

"That means they had another car waiting." says Raf'.

"Yes. They only went two miles before the PTC shows it stopped next to a park at seven minutes after four. I'm downloading your GC's for that location and set your port to arrive five minutes before they stopped. You'll only have seconds to get a PTC on their new vehicle, E'."

"Copy that." says Raf'.

One minute later Madison, Ethan and Rafael have ported to that park. Several vehicles are parked on the side street so they crouch behind a large hedge and wait to see which vehicle the kidnappers will use. Ethan's already got DB loaded with a PTC.

"You'll likely have less than fifteen seconds," says Raf, "so have DB flying over those cars now."

"Good thinking, Raf'." says Madison.
It was, because two minutes later the kidnappers race up and stop beside a black van. The man gets out of the car with a now wide awake and blindfolded Sarah, her screams muffled by his hand. With the help of his female accomplice, they get Sarah into

the black van, unaware in the frenzy DB dropped a
PTC onto the van's roof, and a second on the hood.
As the van drives off, DB is following closely taking
video of the licence tag.

"Let's hope the tag's clear for Maya." says Ethan.

"You got two PTC's for her. Great job." says Raf'.

Minutes later the teens are back in present time in a
Meadowlands, New Jersey, restaurant, hoodies up
and shades on, speaking on their DAC's with Maya.

"His van stopped four times for traffic lights
which I saw on the recorded CCTV. There was
one other stop for thirty-two seconds."

"That's long enough to get Sarah in another
vehicle." Raf' says.

"Yes. The PTC's confirm the van hasn't moved in
over thirteen hours. DB's vid was great and I've just
accessed the New Jersey Department of Motor
Vehicles database." She looks at the monitor on her
left which has a screenshot of the van's licence tag
from DB's video. She enters the digits into the Motor
Vehicle 'Search' bar on her other monitor and
seconds later a photo and I.D. of the registered
owner of the black van fills the screen. She reads
aloud for her friends 7,811 miles away.

"The van is registered to Jerry Stevens, thirty-two.
He lives in an apartment building ..." she taps a
few keys and the screenshot of the van is replaced by
a Google Earth image of an apartment building,
"where the van's been parked for thirteen hours."

"Incredible, Maya!" Madison whispers.

"Can you call the FBI?" asks Ethan.

"No, because the van stopped for thirty-two seconds in a residential area, two miles from his apartment."

"That's long enough to get Sarah in another vehicle." Raf' says.

"Yes. We must confirm he's in his apartment before I call the FBI."

"I've got an idea." says Madison. "What does the kidnapper look like, Maya?"

***

Two minutes later Madison, Ethan and Rafael walk in the lobby of the kidnapper's apartment building and get on the elevator. Ethan has a newspaper under his arm. Video glasses on.

"Any questions on what to say, E'?" says Raf'.

"No, keep it casual .. don't look inside when he's looking at me .. try to hear any sound of Sarah and the woman talking."

"Good man." says Raf'. "We'll wait at the elevator. Any problems, shout and I'm there."

The elevator door opens. Ethan takes a calming breath and walks out with them. They note the unit numbers on the wall with arrows pointing in opposite directions. Raf' points to the left. Ethan walks up to number 609. After a calming breath he knocks three times on the door, as Raf' and Madison watch near the elevator. The door opens and Jerry, the kidnapper, looks warily at Ethan.

"What do you want, kid?" sizing him up.

"Hi, sir." Ethan smiles, holding up the newspaper. "My name's Jimmy with the Star-Ledger …"
Jerry looks at the newspaper, and Ethan quickly looks into the apartment, as he continues his spiel. "and we're doing a special for home delivery …"

"Look, kid, this isn't a good time."

"Oh, I'm sorry to bother you, sir. I can come back another time." as a woman's angry, muffled voice can be heard.

"No!" he snaps, slamming the door shut. Ethan runs back to the elevator and Rafael opens the door to the stairs. They hustle down two flights to the fourth floor landing. Ethan's excited, breathing fast.

"He's the guy you described! … he was really nervous! Then I heard a woman's voice and a young girl crying. I let on I didn't hear. I couldn't hear what the woman was saying, but she was defo angry, and it really spooked him."

"Great job, E'!" says Madison'.

"Yeah, man!" says Raf'. "You can call the FBI, Maya."

"First I have to scrub the video outside and inside the building because they'll be looking at everything. I'll need fifteen minutes to access the info I need to do that. You guys go across the street and make sure they don't leave."

"Copy that." says Raf'.

It took Maya fourteen minutes to complete her video scrubbing, and then she made her anonymous call to the New Jersey Police Department, using an AI-Voice generator to make her sound like a middle-aged male with a New Jersey accent.

Fifteen minutes later a dozen FBI and New Jersey State troopers are leading Jerry Stevens and his female accomplice in handcuffs from the building. Two female Agents and two Paramedics assist an emotional Sarah inside an ambulance. Yellow Crime Scene tape and several State Troopers keep several dozen people outside the perimeter, so no one notices Madison, Ethan and Rafael watching from a distance.

"We likely saved Sarah's life, guys." Raf' says softly, his arm around an emotional Madison, wiping happy tears. "Best day of my life." she sniffs, as they watch the ambulance drive past them with an eleven year old girl inside who will never know the identity of the four teens who selflessly reunited her with her family.

Maya is watching this on her monitor, via the live feed from the teens' video glasses. "And there will be many more." she says, tissuing happy tears.

The next morning, the Giller's are having breakfast.

"I'm glad you're feeling better, dear." says mom.

"It was very good of you, E'." says dad.

"Mad' would do the same for me." he shrugs.

"How was the rest of your day?" Madison asks.

"We snorkelled again, and had a great dinner at a restaurant the tour operator recommended."

"Next time we go back you'll come." mom says. "Oh, what's this?" she grabs the TV remote and pumps the volume, as Madison looks at Ethan.

Lyla Wiggons is at the News Desk with a text Chyron on the TV screen: *Anonymous Tip Saves Kidnapped New Jersey Girl*.

"It's always so nice to report good news," says Lyla, "and last night the parents of eight year old Sarah Hoskins, who was kidnapped very early Saturday morning from her home in Meadowlands, New Jersey, spoke with the media to express their heartfelt thanks for Sarah's safe return."
Lyla is replaced on screen by video of Sarah's mother and father, flanked by uniformed Police and Detectives. The father reads a prepared statement.

"I don't know if there's words that can adequately express our joy and thanks to the New Jersey FBI and Police who were so compassionate during our nightmare. There's no words to describe the horror we experienced seeing our daughter kidnapped and driven away." he pauses to compose himself. "We may never know who called in with the tip that led to the apartment where Sarah was being held, but if you are watching, my wife and I are forever indebted to you for your courage in acting on whatever it was you saw that led you to call the FBI. God Bless you."

Madison is teary eyed as she gets up and walks out of the kitchen.

"Isn't that wonderful." says mom.

"Yeah, good people." says dad, as Ethan gets up and leaves the kitchen. When he gets to the hall he runs up the stairs and knocks softly on Madison's bedroom door. She opens it and he walks in. She closes the door and hugs him tightly.

Moments later Rafael is in his bedroom, looking at the video of Mr. Hoskins.

"… if you are watching, my wife and I are forever indebted to you for your courage in acting on whatever it was you saw that caused you to call the FBI. God Bless you." Rafael is emotional…

In Mumbai, Maya has just watched the video and is wiping happy tears. She picks up her cell phone and looks at Madison and Ethan smiling at her.

"My heart is bursting with joy." says Maya.

"Ours' as well, Maya." says Madison. "I wrote down what you said when we talked about Maria." Reads from her journal. "Vasudhaiva Kutumbakam the world is one family. It's true, we're all connected, Maya."

Rafael is on the call, too.

"Clive Borges … Mrs. Gonzalez … now Sarah."

"And the doctors in Africa …" says Maya.

"It all began with Maria …" Madison says softly.

"Vasudhaiva Kutumbakam …" Maya says.

19. $5 MILLION REWARD!

The next week was uneventful for the teens. Madison and Ethan had classes and Mad' had soccer practices and another pre-season match which they won 4-1. Rafael worked four day shifts and one midnight shift, and Maya was busy with her day job with the Space Agency, while on call 24-7 with the Intelligence Agency. They were also searching online every day for their next case, but it wasn't easy finding a crime where the Police had few leads that occurred within the past twenty-four hours.

It's a sunny Thursday morning and Madison and Ethan are having breakfast with dad.

"Mom suggested we do a weekend in Melbourne so we can do the Great Barrier Reef tour."

"That'd be great." says Madison. "Just have to come up with a good excuse for 'Bec and Nat'."

"Oh, what's this?" says dad, reacting to the TV News. On the screen in big letters: *Billion Dollar Gold Heist.* Lyla Wiggons is reporting.

"The FBI reports they have very few leads in last night's daring gold bullion robbery in Kentucky. The Bank's shipment was being transported in an armored vehicle which was inside a transport truck when thieves, posing as police officers at a staged accident scene, overpowered the guards and made off with the truck. Fortunately the guards were released unharmed near the robbery. The F.B.I. are hopeful the Bank's five million dollar reward will lead to arrests."

Madison shoots a look at Ethan, who subtly holds up five fingers and silently mouths 'five million.'

"Good the guards weren't harmed." says dad, standing up. He kisses Madison on the cheek.

"Have a great day, guys, and give some thought to the Reef Tour."

"Okay, Dad." says Madison, as he exits. They wait for the door to close, then -

"Five million, Mad'! Let's call Maya!" They run out of the kitchen.

It's seven o'clock in the evening and Maya is having dinner with her parents. "Have you spoken with Madison and Ethan this week?" Sanjay asks. Before Maya can answer her phone pings. Her parents know what this means. Without a word, Maya glides her wheelchair down the spotless, wood floor and enters her room. She closes the door and quickly activates the sliding door as she motors to her desk. Her fingers move rapidly across her keyboard and in seconds Madison and Ethan appear on the monitor to her left.

"Hey, Maya, got a minute?" says Madison.

"Yes, of course."

"You hear about the Gold bullion robbery last night in Kentucky?"

"Yes, but I don't know the details."

"There's a five million dollar reward."

"Which is like a *trillion* Rupees." grins Ethan.

"Isn't it too big for us?"

"All we have to do is port back to the robbery and have DB drop a PTC on the truck and you track where they went." says Madison. "We go there, confirm the gold is there and we tip-off the FBI."

"Five million dollars would help a lot of people." says Maya. "Let me pull up Raf's schedule." looking at her second monitor which displays *Raf's Shifts This Week*. "He's working a midnight shift." She looks at the big clocks on the wall and focuses on the one below *Majorca* showing it's two o'clock there now.

The clock in the Majorca gym is showing 2:03. Rafael does his kick-box training here three days a week, and today he's sparring with a guy with a lot of energy. Rafael puts his hands up for a break.

"Nico, you're too aggressive, man."

"But you're so good, Raf', I gotta try an' catch you off guard, man."

"Nico, if some guy comes up to you on the street, he doesn't know if you can take care of yourself, and …" his phone pings. "I gotta take this." he runs off..

Two minutes later, Madison and Ethan are on Maya's monitor, looking at Rafael on her other monitor.

"Our window to go back is three in the morning Majorca time, so we'd have to go earlier." says Maya.

"We can skip classes." says Ethan.

"And my match doesn't start till four-thirty."

"Okay, guys, are we agreed this will be our next case?" Maya asks.

"Yeah, let's do it." says Raf, his game face on.

"Okay, Raf, we'll be on on the beach in twenty." Madison says, and she and Ethan vanish from the monitor screen. Rafael is still on the other monitor.

"This could be dangerous, Raf'. Please keep them safe."

"I will, Maya." he nods, and his screen goes dark. Maya takes her beads from her desk and closes her eyes in a silent Prayer for her friends.

* * *

The Hamptons is on the east end of Long Island, New York, and is a popular vacation destination for the very wealthy. One of its part-time residents is fifty year old billionaire Wesley Kynsor, who spends a few Summer months here at his forty million dollar mansion. He is a collector of fine artworks by Picasso and Rembrandt, among others. He's also a brilliant musician, and in addition to the artworks displayed on his walls are portraits of his personal heroes; Mozart. Beethoven. Napoleon. President Kennedy, and the framed movie poster of his favorite film,

"Iron Man". He's never been married, and the only person he trusts is his long-time personal assistant, Helga, also aged 50.

Kynsor has never granted the media an interview, and he has not been photographed in over thirty years. His silky, grey hair reaches his shoulders when it's not in a ponytail. Deeply tanned, he has never smoked, consumed alcohol or drugs of any type, and he follows a rigid exercise regimen overseen by Team Kynsor's personal trainers. His real name is Herb Schlosky, born in Philadelphia to parents who gave him up for adoption at birth, and he was raised in numerous Orphanages. No one knows how he made his fortune, and the F.B.I. certainly are not aware that he is the mastermind behind the gold bullion robbery! This morning Kynsor is swimming in his pool, showing form that would make Michael Phelps proud, under the scrutiny of his two male, personal trainers. Helga is with them, dressed conservatively in a grey suit and black loafers, hair pulled back in a bun, and no makeup. Kynsor gets out of the pool and a trainers wraps a white robe around him, as Helga approaches holding her phone and a clown mask in her other hand.. "Lopez." she says crisply. Kynsor nods and takes the phone, holding it with the screen pointed towards the ground so his face won't be visible on the video call with Lopez, 40's, with a moustache and glasses.

"Has the inventory been secured?" holding a

voice distorter device to his throat.

"Yes, sir. And the FBI say they have no leads."

"So they say! Likely to get us to drop our guard." he nods to Helga and she holds the clown mask over her face as she speaks.

"Destroy your phone immediately, and use burner phone three for your next call."
She ends the call and walks to Kynsor, who's looking to the skies.

"I'm getting a troubling feeling, Helga."

"Lopez, sir?"

"No … I can't explain it."

"Perhaps a performance would provide clarity, sir?"

"Yes! Schedule it after my Grigorski call."

"Very good, sir."

* * *

Twenty minutes after their call, Madison and Ethan are with Rafael at their secluded spot on the Majorca beach. It's four hundred yards from *Sergio's* where they had breakfast three months ago, and later told Rafael how they teleported there in seconds from their Florida home. Now they are about to use Dr. G's incredible invention to help the FBI capture the robbers of one billion dollars of gold bullion!

"The guards reported the robbery took place at five minutes past ten last night. The fake police likely arrived at least fifteen minutes before to set up the car accident." says Maya, her words heard via their DAC's. "So I've programmed you to get there thirty minutes before, to give you time to find a safe place to observe them."

"Copy that." says Madison.

"Police didn't learn of the robbery for two hours." says Maya. "The closest airport is only 19 miles from the robbery. That means they could have got the gold onto a jet within an hour and flown it anywhere. And there's another airport an hour away."

"That's likely what they did." says Rafael.

"If the robbers see us, you know the drill, guys." says Madison.

"Big inhale then exhale while we run." says Ethan, looking at Rafael.

"And hit the launch key." he says.

"Let's hope you don't have to." says Maya.

"You ready, guys?" They nod their heads.

"We're goin' dark." says Ethan.

Rafael looks in all directions to make sure no one is watching them. They kneel down, inhale deeply, then forcefully exhale all the oxygen they can from their lungs. They tap the 'Launch' key and a second later … they've vanished!

* * *

The gold bullion robbery went down on a two-lane highway in a remote, rural area. Madison, Ethan and Rafael have just arrived from their 4,557 mile flight from the Majorca beach, which took all of eleven seconds. It's a cool evening, so they pull up their black hoodies to cover their heads. They're two hundred and fifty feet from the two-lane road, which is just inside DB's three hundred feet range to drop a PTC. They're sitting behind tall, thick trees and many bushes, with their video glasses on.

"Why does the bank have all this gold bullion, E'? asks Rafael.

"Ask Mad', she's been studying it."

"The history of gold's amazing, Raf'. For 100's of years it actually had no value - it was just prized for its' beauty."

"I never knew that."

"Yeah, early civilizations equated gold with Gods, so it was made into objects of worship."

"When did people start using gold as money?"

"Around 700 B.C. merchants produced the first known coins. They were sixty-three per cent gold and twenty-seven per cent silver, and were called electrum."

"Hey, dude, got change for an Electrum?" grins Ethan.

"This is very interesting." says Raf.

"Yeah, it's cool when you think how people lived hundred's of years ago, and realize everything we have today is the result of them." Madison says.

"The Wright brothers first flight was only 12 seconds, Raf," says Ethan. "and sixty-six years later

Neil Armstrong walked on the Moon."

"Amazing! So how big are these gold bars, E'?"

"I went online to check. Each bar weighs twenty-seven pounds, and they're about seven inches, by three and a half, by one and a half." using his hands to convey the length, height and width. Madison suddenly reacts to something.

"This must be the fake Police cars." she whispers, her pulse quickening, seeing four vehicles approaching from the East side of the road.

"Oh, geez, my heart's beating outta my chest!" says Ethan, barely getting the words out.

"Take a deep breath, E', and hold it for seven seconds." Rafael says calmly. Ethan does as told, and exhales. "Again." Rafael says. Madison's nerves have kicked in, too, and she's taking breaths.

"Guys, they're not gonna see us." says Raf'.

"We're gonna get great vid for Maya with our VG's. Mad' and I will focus on faces and licence tags. You get DB ready with the PTC's." Ethan takes DB from his hoodie pocket and two small ziplock bags.

Two Police cruisers and the two vehicles in the 'accident' now block both lanes of the road. The Police vehicles' flashing lights eerily pierce the darkness, as four fake Police Officers stand with four men involved in the accident.

"They've set up the car accident." whispers Madison, her heart beating faster than before any penalty kick she's ever had.

"It should be going down any minute!" whispers Raf, looking left towards the road where he knows the Gold bullion truck will be coming from. "Here they come!"

Two Police cruisers escorting the transport truck slow down and stop ahead of the transport, which has no signage. Two Police Officers get out and signal for the driver to remain in the truck cab, while the other two Officers remain outside their vehicle. The Officers walk towards the fake police officers who have their backs to them. Suddenly they turn around with guns drawn and Halloween masks covering their faces. Two fake Officers keep their guns trained on the real Officers, while the other two and the four accident drivers, their faces also covered by masks, rush towards the transport with guns drawn. The two Officers outside their cruiser are outnumbered and wisely raise their hands above their heads.

The teens are mesmerized watching the drama unfold. "This is really well-organized." whispers Rafael.

"Just like in the movies." whispers Ethan.

"Took a lot of planning." says Rafael.

"Ready for DB?" Ethan looks at Raf, who nods.

"Get some good vid for Maya." whispers Ethan, who presses a few numbers on his keypad and DB flies off, its black body blending into the darkness. DB soars over the transport where two men have just affixed self-sticking, six feet by six feet signs on each side of the transport - *California Produce* - and didn't notice DB dropping a PTC' on the roof.

The four real Police Officers - now blindfolded, and wrists secured behind their backs with plastic zip ties - are being led off the road by the robbers who put up the signage. "What are they doing, Raf?" Madison barely whispers, afraid even the slightest sound could carry over to the men now only 100 feet away and still walking! Ethan's eyes are wide and his heart rate must be at a lifetime high as he looks at Rafael, who puts his finger to his lips, his eyes riveted on the men who are partly obscured by the bushes' lush foliage. They're not coming directly towards them, but still a very close seventy-five feet off to their right where they stop beside a clump of similar bushes. One of the robbers places something to his throat, which distorts his voice. He's close enough so the teens can hear.

"We're not going to harm you. Stay here until help comes. We have a drone watching you. If you attempt to get help we will know." The two men run away quickly to the six robbers waiting for them in the idling vehicles.

Madison and Ethan watch the transport truck drive off, escorted by the real Police cars, as Rafael looks to the dark skies in all directions. He puts his finger to his lips and hand motions them to quietly stand up. They follow his lead and walk slowly, fearful the sound of a step on a small twig could crackle through the still night air and reach the bound Officers who believe they are miles from another human. After gingerly walking over two hundred yards the teens kneel down.

"Think there's a drone watching?" Ethan asks.

"I didn't see one. I think they wanted them to believe it so they'd stay put."

"They did for five hours before they were rescued." Madison says.

"Okay, let's get back to PT so Maya can check our vid." says Raf'.

***

A few minutes later Maya is looking closely at the video playing on the monitor to her left that she just downloaded from Madison and Rafael's video glasses. It's very dark, the only light provided by the flashing lights of the fake Police cruisers. Maya looks at the monitor on her right where Madison and Rafael's faces fill the screen, coming live directly from Ethan's video glasses.

"Great work with DB, Ethan. The PTC's are sending a strong signal, and he got me a good look at the faces of the two men putting the signs on the transport."
She angles her monitor so they can see the faces of the two men we saw earlier.

"Good. Maybe it'll help us connect them in the next few days." says Raf.

"What's your hunch?" asks Madison. "Think they

flew it out from an airport last night before it was reported stolen?"

"No, it's too risky. The FBI will have Agents at all airports." Raf' says.

"I agree." Maya says, looking at her monitor where the flashing red dot is not moving now.

"Guys, the transport has stopped for the first time. I'll source the location." Her fingers tap the keyboard and an address pops on the screen.

"I got the address … let's see what it is." Several keystrokes and then a Google Earth static view of a large warehouse appears on her screen.

"The transport stopped at a warehouse twenty-seven miles from the robbery."

"So we can tip off the FBI?" asks Ethan.

"Not yet." says Maya.

"Why?" asks Madison.

"Because the masterminds behind this won't be there, and my hunch is the gold wasn't there very long. They would have got the truck off the road quickly before the robbery was reported because they know the FBI will have Agents checking every airport and warehouse within a two hour drive."

"I agree, Maya. In my training I learned a lot about how criminals think. We need to port back to last night and check that warehouse."

"I'm getting your GC's, guys." tapping her keyboard.

"We're goin' back in time .. to solve the crime."

says Ethan.

"How many tracking chips do you have left, E?" asks Rafael.

"Uh, two regular and two PTC's."

"That's it? says Raf. "We need a lot more."

"You'll have to go home." says Madison.

"How many should I get, Raf'?"

"Fifteen of each, to be safe."

"Hurry, E." says Madison.

"I downloaded your GC's to the warehouse, Ethan. There's a security fence around it, so you guys are going to the roof."

Fifty-six seconds later Ethan has ported back to PT, which is Friday morning, almost eleven hours after the robbery they are investigating seven hundred and twenty-three miles away. As Ethan runs into the kitchen he's stunned seeing mom making breakfast.

"Mom?! W-what're you home for?" he stammers, as mom smiles. "My annual checkup. Why aren't you at school?"
Mad', Raf', Maya and me are tracking the gold bullion robbery last night.

"Uh, I, I forgot some papers … in the lab." he stammers.

"Did dad tell you we're thinking of going to Melbourne for a weekend?"

"Yeah, it's a great idea." walking towards the hall.

"The Reef is massive … twelve hundred miles long."

"That's what Mad' said."

"It takes almost two hours by boat to get there."

"Really? Uh, Mom I really have to get back."

"Oh, sure."

Ethan dashes downstairs and runs to a large cabinet and opens it. He opens a plastic container and carefully counts out a bunch of tiny tracking chips and slides them into a small ziplock bag and seals it. He opens a clear plastic container and carefully pours a white, gooey substance into a larger ziplock bag. He seals it, closes the cabinet, and dashes up the stairs. He walks in the kitchen, expecting mom to be there. She's not.

"Mom!?" calling out.

"I'm getting in the shower, E'."

Ethan smiles and rolls up his sweater and quickly activates the sliding panel on his cast-sleeve as he runs outside.

A minute later Ethan is on the warehouse roof with Madison and Rafael, kneeling behind the A.C. Unit. He's carefully handing tracking chips to Rafael, who puts them in his pocket. Suddenly the sound of a door opening and closing shatters the eerie stillness of the night. *Have they been* seen? Rafael puts his fingers to his lips. Madison looks at Ethan, who's more terrified than her. Suddenly the flame from a lighter silhouettes part of the big dude's face as he sates his nicotine needs, expelling a waft of smoke into the air. Madison and Ethan exhale in relief as

Raf' motions them to stay here, zipping his lips. He stands up and walks towards the guard thirty feet away, his back to Raf'.

"Hey, you shouldn't be up here!" says Rafael sternly. The Guard turns around.

"Who are you?" sizing up Rafael.

"Put it out right now! We're going back inside." The Guards drops his cigarette and heels it into the cement. He looks warily at Rafael as he opens the door. Rafael follows him inside.

Madison and Ethan are watching.

"That was amazing how Raf' took control!" grins Ethan.

"He can hear you."

"Great job, Raf'."

Rafael is following the Guard walking down the stairs, so he can't reply to Madison and Ethan via the DAC in his right ear. They reach the main floor and the Guard opens the door. As they walk in Rafael's eyes dart left, then right. He speaks in a whisper, lips not moving, fingers of his right hand flicking near his mouth as if he's scratching an itch.

"Transport still here … off-loading boxes to small vans … at least ten … they're moving it out of here … get PTC's ready, E. "

"Hey, who are you?" a male voice booms. Rafael looks to his right and approaches the speaker, a big guy, late 30's, sizing him up, his huge biceps too big for his t-shirt. *He's one of the guys who put the signs on the truck*. His friends call him Drew.

"Who told the guard he could go on the roof for a smoke?" Rafael snaps.

"And you are?!" Drew's sneer is bigger.

"Answer my question!" his eyes locked on Drew.

"Let's take this in my office." Drew says curtly and walks off.

As Rafael follows, his eyes are darting less now because he can't be certain if others are watching him. He follows Drew into an office and the door is closed by another guy with similar biceps and attitude. *The other sign guy.*

"You gonna answer my question now?! Rafael snaps, eyes fixed on Drew.

"Not until you tell me who you are!" glaring back.

"Okay, I'll tell you!" leaning on Drew's desk, still glaring. "I'm the guy making sure no one's helping themselves to a sample of the merch (gold bars). Did anyone pat him down before he went to the roof? Maybe he tossed it … come back later for it. Nice overtime, huh?"

"Every guy here was checked out! How come I've never seen you before?" eyes not moving from Rafael. "For all I know, you got on the roof to try to steal a few bars."

"Got on the roof?" Rafael grins. "Like Captain America?"

"I never saw you come in! Did you, Josh?" Josh shakes his head. Drew looks at Rafael. "So, either you tell me who you are, and who sent you, or I'm making a phone call. What's it gonna be!?"

"Okay, I'll save you the call." He turns, looking like he's deep in thought. Then he looks at Josh. "Do you know how many people there are in the world, Josh?"

"Okay, now you're wasting my time!" snaps Drew, reaching for his phone.

"No, I'm not, you'll see." looking at Drew. Then he looks at Josh to get his answer.

Josh shrugs. "I dunno, at least six billion, I think."

"Not a bad guess, Josh. But there's over eight billion." Now Rafael looks at Drew. "How many of those eight billion people do you think know the signs that *you two guys* put on the transport were for *California Produce*?"
The look on Drew's stunned face blares *This guy's for real*! and his macho demeanor is flushed as Rafael looks at Josh to get his reaction. Ditto.

"Alright, now let's get out there and see how they're doing!" Rafael snaps and walks to the door. Josh quickly opens it and Rafael walks out, followed by the stunned guys. Drew jogs to catch up to Rafael, who's looking closely at the activity, not caring now who's looking at him.

"Sorry about that, man. Can't be too careful. Uh, I'm Drew." offering his hand with a respectful smile. Rafael offers his hand with a nano second look - that's all Drew's getting - because his focus is on the workers taking the twenty-seven pound gold bars out of the armoured truck. They hand the bars two at a time to others who place them into wooden crates about the size and depth of a suitcase. Then two workers place the loaded crate on a metal table with wheels and roll it to a van and stow it. Rafael's video glasses are capturing great vid of this, as well as the licence tags of as many vans in his clear view. He's a few steps ahead of Drew, and he covers his mouth as he whispers.

"PTC's ready, E'?"

"Yes." his voice crackles in Raf's right ear.

"How'd you stay so calm, man?" in awe.

"Jason Bourne couldn't have done it better!" says Madison.

"Be careful, guys." he whispers, then he turns to Drew. "Have the vans been checked for tracking devices?"

"Uh, no. I guess we should, huh?" He watches Rafael walk towards the vans lined up in a long row. As he reaches the first van Rafael kneels down to look at the underside, pretending to look for a small device that would be secured by a magnet to the chassis. As he stands up and leans inside for a look he casually takes one of Ethan's tiny tracker chip from his jeans pocket and tosses it under the seat.

"This one's good to go." slapping the roof twice, looking at Drew, who nods, clearly impressed at Rafael's thoroughness as Rafael jogs to the next van.

Ten minutes later the last van is driving slowly out of the warehouse, watched by Rafael and Drew.

"Is there a washroom on this floor?"

"Yeah, but it's backed up." Drew says. "You'll have to use the one upstairs."

"Be right back." he jogs to the stairs door. "I'm coming up now, guys, we're getting out of here." he whispers, looking pleased. He dashes up the stairs two at a time and heads down the hallway. He's quickly on the roof, where Madison and Ethan have their sleeves rolled up, ready to launch.

"Did you get PTC's on all of them, E'?"

"Every one."

"Great work! I got chips inside six vans. What's PT in Majorca now, Mad'?"

"Your shift starts in two and a half hours. My match starts in an hour, so E' and I have to get home now."

"Maya, I'll keep my DAC in during my shift in case you have any updates.

"Copy that."

* * *

Back at Kynsor's mansion in the Hamptons it's noon on Friday, the day after the gold bullion robbery. Kynsor is on a large stage, a bright spotlight shining on him, as he plays Bach - Partita No. 2, Chaconne, on his four million dollar Stradivarius Violin. He's a world class talent. Helga is sitting in plush, theater seats with Kynsor's chefs, maids, gardeners and personal trainers. Kynsor finishes with a flourish and stands. Helga quickly presses a button on a TV remote and the sound of thousands of people clapping and cheering fills the small auditorium, along with the applause of his staff, standing now.

"Bravo! Bravo!" Kynsor bows to his fans, basking in their adulation.

* * *

Seventy-four seconds after launching from the warehouse roof, Madison and Ethan are running inside their kitchen and going straight to the 'fridge.

"I'm so thirsty and hungry!" Madison says, opening a bottle of water and guzzling it down, as her brother does the same.

"Ohhhh, that's sooo good!" he says, grabbing a package of muffins. He tears it open and hands Madison one. She takes a bite as her cell on the island counter buzzes. She picks it up. "Hey Bec.'

"Why'd you skip class? I called and text you a bunch."

"I woke up with a bad stomach." chewing the muffin.

"So you're not playing?"

"No, I'll be there in twenty. Gotta go!" another big bite, and as she chews, "I really hate telling all these LWL's." (Little White Lies)

"Tracking gold bullion robbers isn't an option." Opening a jug of milk and pouring a tall glass, which he drains in six seconds. "Glad I don't have to run around kicking a ball for two hours."

"Hope it's raining hard by half-time and they call it," another bite of muffin, "or I may have to fake leg cramps."
They react to the front door opening and Madison looks down the hall at mom.

"Hey, Mom. How'd your appointment go?" hugging her.

"Fine. All set for your match?"

"Yeah, just heading out with E' now."

* * *

Rafael has just arrived home from his very long day. Papa is in the kitchen, standing at the stove. The clock on the wall shows 9:05pm.

"Where were you, Rafael? You didn't answer your phone. I was worried."
Sorry I had to go to Kentucky in the US for a few hours

"Sorry, papa, I misplaced my phone. What's for dinner? I'm starved." smiling.
I really need to lie down for two hours.

* * *

It's just after four o'clock on Saturday morning in Mumbai. Maya is in her pink robe, seated at the desk in her home office. She's on a Zoom with Khan and Courtnall. Maya's monitor displays two lines of gibberish - letters, numbers and every symbol above

the numbers on a keypad. As her fingers flash across
the keypad, new lines of text appear below the
gibberish which are very easy to read for a normal
human. Maya reads them aloud;

"The first line says; *transfer received today.* The
line below says *noodles and sauce await courier.*"

"Excellent, Maya." says Courtnall.

"Sorry we had to waken you, Maya. Get some
sleep." says Khan.

"I'm glad I was able to help." stifling a yawn.

"Goodnight." and she exits the Zoom.

What Khan and Courtnall don't know is they didn't
waken Maya. She's been up for two hours tracking
the movement of the vans loaded with the gold
bullion. Her fingers flash across the keypad and now
her other monitor is divided into four squares, each
one displaying recorded CCTV video of sparse
vehicle traffic on those four area roads. Maya's eyes
dart from each square, searching for the vans she
knows began leaving the warehouse ten hours ago.

She turns quickly to her other monitor and in
seconds her keystrokes bring up a map that fills the
screen. There's twelve *flashing* **red dots** spread out
across the screen, each one a van that has a tracking
device DB dropped onto its roof. And six of the
vans have a Tracker Chip placed inside by Rafael,
enabling Maya to track the vans' 'live' movement.

"Where are you all going?" she says softly. Then

she looks at the clocks on the wall, her focus the two
that are side-by-side, showing the current time is just
after midnight in Majorca, and just after six o'clock
on Friday evening in Merritt Island.

"It would be so much easier if we were all in the
same Time-Zone." she says wearily. "They must
be so tired." stifling another yawn.

* * *

It's half-time in the *Rebels* first game of the new
season. The girls are in the locker room taking on
fluids and munching orange slices. Madison is
rubbing her left calf muscle with her right hand as
she drinks from a juice bottle. Coach Jamieson walks
in. "How's the cramp, Mad'?"

"I'm good, Coach." Madison says. It's the first lie
she's told in months that doesn't make her feel bad.

Moments later, it's just prior to the start of the
second half. Ethan is walking on the sidelines
speaking via his DAC to his sister 200 feet away.

"Maya's tracking the vans … they're going to
separate locations."

"Have you heard from Raf'?"

"No. His shift just started."

"He's gonna be exhausted tomorrow."

* * *

After wolfing down papa's delicious Spanish meatballs in garlic sauce, Rafael managed to get two hours of much needed rest. It wasn't real sleep because his brain was still processing the incredible excitement of their fourth case, which was way more exciting than anything he'd experienced in his first months with the Palma Police. Papa roused him thirty minutes before his shift was starting, and a two-minute freezing cold shower - *el iceberg* - had cleared his cobwebs. So he felt surprisingly good as he began his shift with Carlos, walking along Palma's popular promenade by the sea. It was busy as usual this Friday night, with locals enjoying a relaxing stroll in the evening air.

"How was your day, Raf'?"

I was in Kentucky getting evidence on that huge gold bullion robbery.

"Good. Met up with some friends … had a workout. You?"

"Took Catalina to the dentist. Kicked the ball with Sergio. It was good."

"You're a lucky guy, beautiful kids."

* * *

The *Rebels* lead the match 4-2 with three minutes left in the game. Madison scored a nice goal early in the second half, and later made a slick pass to Rebecca for the go-ahead goal. Coach Jamieson, not wanting to risk an injury to last year's Conference leading goal scorer, substituted for Madison with eight minutes left in the match. She was exhausted, and with her DAC still in, was getting an update with Maya.

"What time is it there, Maya?"

"I don't want to look." she says wearily.

"Must be after four a.m." she grimaces.

"I'm canceling my rehab, I can't be offline."

"Hey, guys," says Rafael. "Carlo is talking to some people so I have a minute."

"The gold is in twelve vans still driving in many different directions."

"These guys are very smart. What's your hunch?" Rafael asks.

"I don't have one yet. Most of my cases with stolen property the transaction is concluded quickly. This is not like anything I've seen."

"They don't know we're tracking them, and have access to CCTV wherever they go." says Madison.

"I got a feeling today is going to be a big one."

Maya says, then adds, "*tomorrow* in your case."

"Yeah, I'll need some sleep first." says Raf'

"I wish we were helping save a kid's life, not looking for greedy bad guys." says Mad.

"I hear you, but the five million reward will help a lot of people." Raf' says.

"That's what keeps me going." says Maya.

"We couldn't do this without you." says Madison.

* * *

The next morning Kynsor is in his den, eating from seven plates loaded with hamburgers .. french fries with gobs of ketchup .. lasagna .. pancakes .. potato chips .. M & M's .. and a carton of ice cream. It's quite the visual seeing him take a bite of hamburger and after a few chews he's back into the pancakes with a bunch of french fries. There are ten large, digital clocks side-by-side, in two rows of five, on the wall across from him displaying the current time in the cities identified above them: New York Riyadh London Paris Cairo Buenos Aires Los Angeles Beijing Tokyo Moscow. Below each clock is a 55 inch TV with that city's 'live' news and stock market reports, with the sound muted. He has a mouthful of lasagna as he quickly grabs the TV remote and un-mutes the TV under *New York*. News Anchor Lyla Wiggons is with a man, early 40's, identified by the text at the bottom of the screen; *FBI Special Agent David Kimble*.

"A shipment of this size would require a jet to move the gold quickly, so we've had every airport across the country on high alert since we first learned of the robbery."

Kynsor chuckles as he chews another bite of who knows what.

"The shipment will soon be a lot smaller, Agent Kimble!" laughing at the TV.

"Has the five million dollar reward resulted in any leads?" Lyla asks.

"It's very early in the investigation, Lyla, but

we're confident we'll recover every gold bar, and find the people responsible for this crime."

"You better hurry, Kimble," grabbing a forkful of fries, "by next week it will be untraceable!" he laughs.

* * *

The Giller's are having breakfast watching Lyla Wiggons' interview with Agent Kimble.

"We look forward to your updates, Agent Kimble."

"Why was the Bank moving so much gold?" mom asks.

"They sold their building. It was going to the new location." says dad.

"How can people think they'll get away with so many gold bars?"

"If they're smart they'll melt it down, make it untraceable." says dad.

This gets Madison and Ethan's full attention.

"How would you melt it down?" Madison asks.

"They'd need a furnace that can reach around two thousand degrees Fahrenheit. But they'd have to know what they're doing … if the temperature gets too high the gold will oxidize and there'd be a loss of gold."

Madison sneaks a quick look at her brother.

"We're going to miss you guys today, but it's best you rest your leg.." mom says.

"Yeah, I don't wanna aggravate it."

"It's nice you have some time together." says
Ethan.

"Will you be home for dinner?" asks Madison.

"No, we'll be very late." says mom.

"Okay, have fun." Madison says as she walks out,
followed by Ethan. When they get in the hall they
run upstairs - her leg is just fine!

* * *

It's seven-thirty in the evening in Mumbai. Maya is
on a Zoom with Madison, Ethan and Rafael, who
are on the monitor to her left.

"I had a hunch they were going to move the gold
so I set my alarm for one hour, got up, and checked."
Maya says.

"You did that every hour since we last talked? asks
Madison.

"Yes." stifling a yawn.

"You're amazing." says Madison.

"Thanks, Maya." says Rafael.

"Every van moved to a new location overnight.
Most just a few miles, but four traveled a fair
distance. I'll show you." She turns the monitor so it's
facing her other monitor to her right. Her fingers
flash across the keyboard and then the Google Earth
static map we saw before appears on that monitor.
There's two red dots at the far left of the map, two
on the far right, and eight more dots are scattered
several inches apart in the middle. She points to the

red dots at the far left.

"These two vans drove from Louisville to Maple Grove, two hundred and sixty-seven kilometers, Google says. I reviewed all recorded CCTV and as far as I can determine, they made no stops before getting to Maple Grove about three hours ago.

"You did this with every van? asks Rafael.

"Yes." matter-of-factly. "And these two dots," pointing to the far right on the map, "drove to Colver."

"They're taking great risks … the Police could stop the driver for speeding or some other infraction." says Rafael.

"So guys, the FBI Agent was on TV just now", says Ethan, "and dad said if they were smart they'd melt down the gold to make it untraceable."

"I was thinking that as well." says Maya. "So I searched for businesses that would have furnaces to melt that much gold and there's several across Kentucky, including one in Maple Grove (points to monitor) and one in Colver (points).

"Great work, Maya." says Madison. "I think you're onto something here."

"Why would they only move two vans to each city, and the other eight not very far?" asks Maya.

"Maybe they're going to melt it in small batches?" says Ethan.

"I've got an idea." says Rafael.

* * *

Kynsor is standing in his Den, eyes darting left and right, absorbing the latest News on the ten TV's on the wall. Helga walks up quickly, holding her phone and clown mask. "Lopez, sir." Kynsor directs her to hold the phone to the floor, as he places the voice distorter to his throat.

"I trust my new schedule will not be a problem?"

"No, sir. The four vans have arrived."

"How long before the procedure commences?" cautiously avoiding saying *melting*.

"Two hours, sir."
He nods to Helga, who takes the phone and puts the clown mask over her face.

"We expect a flawless execution today. Any failure will have severe consequences, Lopez."

"You have my assurances." says Lopez, clearly very stressed. "I will keep you appraised of all developments."
Helga abruptly ends the call and tosses the clown mask to the sofa. She walks to Kynsor at the opened French doors that lead to the grounds and pool.

"The process used to melt gold is fascinating, Helga. It requires each gold bar to be placed in a crucible about this size." His hands suggest an object three times the size of a thermos bottle. "The crucible is placed in a furnace precisely maintained at two thousand degrees Fahrenheit. When my bars have been liquified, the gold will be poured into a mould to solidify once again, but this time it will be as a two pound bar which can be easily transported and will be accepted by financial institutions after they perform due diligence to authenticate it"

* * *

Maple Grove is a small town with 3,512 residents. About the only excitement found in these parts comes during football and basketball season when the two Maple Grove High School teams battle it out for bragging rights against teams from other sleepy towns around the Kentucky border. There's a handful of businesses you'd find in similar towns across the country - a few diners, grocery store, pharmacy, a unisex hair salon. It's the kind of Town where nothing happens that would ever be of interest to the national media. But that's about to change, because by the end of this sunny, September Saturday the national media will be dispatching reporters here to cover the most sensational event that's ever happened in these parts.

Ten minutes after their strategy chat with Maya, Madison, Ethan and Rafael are sitting on a bench down the street from Franklin's Furnace Company on the outskirts of Maple Grove. It's a one-story building that's off the beaten track, as the locals say, because the closest business is a hundred yards away on the two-lane road that's in serious need of pothole maintenance.

"You guys port to Colver and look for anything

out of the ordinary."

"Like what?" Ethan asks.

"Men dressed like they don't live there. An expensive vehicle with tinted windows. But do not go inside." he cautions.

Madison and Ethan nod and dash down an alley to find a safe place to launch.

* * *

Franklin's small reception area has a desk and two visitors chairs with faded fabric that were likely acquired when Ronald Reagan was President. The man sitting there is Sam, early 50's. He'd still look blue collar in his Sunday best after shaving the three-day growth he's sporting on his wrinkled face. He looks up as Rafael walks in.

"Can I help, ya?" looking uneasy. Before Rafael can say anything he hears a familiar voice. "Hey man, good to see you!" grins Josh, Drew's muscle-bound security guy, walking up, hand extended. *Okay, keep your cool, you fooled him before.*

"Hey, Josh." shaking hands with no hint of a smile, letting his Team know who it is.

"It's okay, Sam, you can go back." Josh says. Sam gets up and as he walks he sneaks a quick look back at the visitor..

"Everything on schedule?" the visitor asks, stone-face serious.

"Oh, yeah. So where'd you get to the other night? Drew and me were .."

"Both vans are here?" cutting him off, establishing he's way higher up in the criminal enterprise than Josh, who takes note.

"Yeah, and the gold's been off-loaded. Just waitin' for the furnace to hit two grand."

"How long?" eyes fixed on Josh, not blinking.

"'Bout ninety minutes."

"Give me the tour!"

"Sure thing." As they walk to the door Josh grins, "FBI won't be looking in Maple Grove."

Rafael ignores him.

* * *

One of Maya's monitors has 'live' video of Franklin's kilns via Rafael's video glasses. Her other monitor has the Google Earth map we saw before with the red dots. *But now the dots are moving.*

"Raf', there's four vans moving towards Colver! And the other four are heading towards Maple Grove! What are we going to do?

"Where's the washroom, Josh?"

"Out that door .. on your left."

Rafael walks quickly and finds the bathroom, locking the door. He turns on the tap for a distracting noise.

"Mad', E', you guys at Colver yet?"

One hundred and sixty-seven kilometers east of Franklin's, Madison and Ethan have arrived. They're in an abandoned field opposite the Colver smelter's operation, which is the only business on the four acres of land overgrown with weeds.

"Yes, across the street. No sign of the vans, but the facility is large enough they could drive inside. And there's a helicopter pad about fifty yards away."

"Can you see if they have outside security cameras?"

"Where should we look?" she asks.

"Light poles .. and near the front door."

"Why do you want to know?" Ethan asks.

"See if a helicopter was there today. That's how the bosses travel."

"There's boxes on two light poles, and one above the front entrance." Madison says.

"I'll check your VG vid. If boxes are security cameras I'll need twenty minutes to hack in. Maya downloaded the video Madison's video glasses provided to confirm those small boxes were security cameras. She couldn't zoom in close enough to get the name of the supplier, but it only took her four minutes to hack into the smelter's e-mail and find the invoices from their security provider. About ninety seconds to get on their website and confirm the type of system they had installed. And another three minutes to bypass their security protocols. Then she hacked into the smelter's server to access the video recorded today, which is playing now on one of her monitors ... showing two men running towards the copter. It's Drew ... and he's with *Lopez*.

Josh and Rafael are in the back kiln area. Raf's eyes dart right, then left, providing Maya with great video of the operation. He notes how cramped the space is, maybe sixty feet long, forty feet across. The five workers all wear fireproof clothing, masks with eye shields, and thick mitts. Another man is checking the gauges on the dozen kilns lining the far wall.

"Raf', forty-one minutes ago your buddy Drew and another man boarded a helo at Colver's that headed west. Based on a normal velo of two hundred and fifty kilometers, they'll be arriving there within minutes. If you copy, please cough." Rafael coughs.

"Mad', did you and E' get back yet?" Maya asks.

"Yes. We're down the street from Franklin's. What should we do, Maya?"

"Stay where you are, and let me know when you see a helicopter landing."

"Copy that."

Madison and Ethan are sitting on a bench in town.

"I'm hungry. I'm gonna check out the variety store. Want anything, Mad'?"

"A juice and an energy bar, thanks. Don't be long … and pull your hoodie up." Ethan jogs across the street, doing as instructed.

* * *

Maya is watching 'live' video of the workers inside the Colver smelter's operation via their security monitoring system, which costs them one hundred and eighty-five dollars every month, the invoices revealed. The operation is quite similar to the video on her other monitor, via Raf's video glasses, where Josh is speaking to Rafael, with the busy Franklin workers behind him.

"Word came down this morning they wanted to speed up the process, but I assume you know that?" Josh says, which doesn't get a response, because Maya's excited voice crackles in Rafael's right ear.

"Raf, I hacked into the power company's server and located Colver's account. I can disconnect their power to shut down their furnaces. If you want me to do it now, cough once." Rafael coughs.

"Okay, I'm shutting them down!"

Down the road from Franklin's, Madison is taking the last bite of her energy bar when suddenly there's a roar. She and Ethan look up and see the helicopter Drew and Lopez boarded earlier.

"Raf, I think Drew's helicopter is landing. Oh, code red, guys!" Then calmly, "Hey Mom, you guys having fun?"

"Yes, I called your cell's, I'm glad you're porting, where'd you …?

"I can't hear you. How was the snorkelling?" cutting her off.

"Fabulous. Now we're off to Rome for dinner, and we wanted to see if …?

"Uh, maybe." cutting mom off. "Gotta go!"

Fifty meters behind the Franklin factory Drew and Lopez duck their heads as the whirling blades of the helicopter kicks up a storm of debris. They get to the rear doors and take a quick look behind to ensure no eyes are on them before going inside.

Rafael and Josh are watching the workers check the temperature gauges on the kilns, while others each place a gold bar in every crucible.

"Raf, Drew and his friend just entered the building from the rear door. Please cough if you copy."
Rafael coughs as Drew and Lopez walk up behind them. From Drew's surprised look seeing Rafael, we know it didn't occur to Josh to let Drew know their buddy, *whatever his name is,* is here.

"Hey, man, how are you?" Drew says all friendly, hand extended for a shake.

"Good." with just the hint of a smile, shaking .

"I assume you two have met?" glancing to Lopez, then back to Rafael.

"No, what's your name?" Lopez asks with zero warmth, sizing up Rafael.

"You don't need to know." he snaps, staring him down.

"Uh, he works for the Boss." says Drew.

"Really? You're pretty young to be playing in this league." clearly suspicious.

"I had my doubts when we met after the robbery,

but he knew about the California Produce signs."
This appeases Lopez a lot. "Oh, okay, I'm Lopez."
offering his hand.

"I know." Rafael says with a slight smile. "Good
to meet you. So, we've got a busy day ahead. I need
the washroom." he walks away.

"That boy sure don't lack for confidence!" grins
Drew. "He said the Boss had him checking to make
sure no one was taking a gold bar for overtime."

"The Boss is a very scary man, Drew. I don't
know his name. He's never shown his face, and he
speaks with a voice distorter. His assistant told me
this morning and failure will have severe
consequences."

"I don't like the sound of that." Drew takes a
nervous breath.

Rafael closes the door to the washroom and locks
it. He turns on the tap and water noisily flows.

"What's happening in Colver?" he whispers.

"Total panic! They have no power and they're
freaking out!"

"Great work! We don't have to worry about that
gold."

"Do you think Lopez bought your story?"

"I think so."

"Let's not take any chances, Raf'." Madison
suggests. "I say get out of there and Maya calls the
FBI"

"Before I do I need to shut off the power there,
which will take me twenty minutes. Then I have to

erase all the video of Raf there, exterior and interior. That will take me ten minutes. Then I need to do the same with the video on Main Street where you guys were talking, because the FBI will be looking at everything."

"You need do Colver, too." says Ethan. "We were across the street and I was in the variety store."

"Hey, man, we got a big problem!" Josh calls from the hall.

"Be right out, Josh." Then he whispers. "I don't know what's happening, guys, don't do anything until I find out, Maya."

"Copy that." she says.

Rafael splashes water on his face and paper towels it dry. He opens the door and Josh is there, looking very anxious. "Drew and Lopez need you in the office."

"What happened?"

"I don't know, man, but Lopez is freaking out!" Walking with Josh across the kiln floor, Rafael's mind is racing. *Are they onto me? Did Lopez phone the Boss?* He takes quick glances towards the workers. *How much time before they begin to melt the gold?* He puts his right hand to his mouth and coughs to hide his whisper. "They may be onto me guys." just before he walks into the office, where Lopez is on the phone, and Drew rushes up to him, very agitated.

"They just lost power at Colver!"

"What?!" says Rafael looking aghast and angry.

"Lopez just called the Boss to tell him." Drew

says to Rafael, who's looking at Lopez.

"No, it just shut down, sir." says Lopez. Seeing Rafael he puts the call on speaker. Kynsor is furious with Lopez, his voice distorted.

"Why didn't you have a backup generator?!" Kynsor screams.

"I'm sorry, sir. I didn't think of it." he looks at Rafael and points to the phone as if to say, *could you talk to him for me?* Raf shakes his head. Then -

"I warned you there'd be severe consequences, Lopez!" snaps Helga.

"B-b-but, it was out of my …? the call is terminated. Lopez looks at Rafael. "It just shut down!" he screams. "And they were at 1900! You heard her, I think the boss is gonna kill me!"

"Was it a power failure in the area?" Raf snaps.

"No, just the factory!! Could you talk to him for me? Maybe he'll listen to you!"

"Sure, but first we have to come up with a solution." He begins to pace like he's considering all options. Lopez and Drew watch, praying this kid can come up with a miracle solution. Rafael looks at them. "Okay … I think we have to assume Colver's power won't be back on today!"

"I think you're right." says Lopez.

Oh, I can guarantee it won't be restored.

"We need to get their gold here as soon as possible, but it's too risky to have six vehicles bring it here. I'll stay here and supervise the initial melting. You guys," looking at Drew and Josh, "go with

Lopez on the helo and load it up."

"I like it!" says Lopez.

"We won't be able to get all the gold on the helo." says Drew, looking at Lopez. "I know, we'll rent a truck."

"Josh, tell the pilot you're going now." says Rafael, "and ask him what his max load is, we don't want to risk your lives." Josh nods to Rafael and runs out. Lopez smiles as he offers his hand to Rafael. "You're a smart guy." they shake hands.

"We play this right, I won't have to call the Boss for you." says Raf', oozing confidence that would make Carlos proud.

"I would be very grateful." says Lopez.

"Okay, man, see you in a couple!" says Drew to Rafael, and he and Lopez rush out of the office. Rafael closes the door and locks it.

"You get that, Maya?"

"Yes, you were amazing!"

"Wait twenty before shutting power here, Maya."

"Copy."

"When do we tip off the FBI?" Madison asks.

"We can't yet. There's gonna be gold in the helo, gold in the truck, and gold in the vans. We need PTC's on the helo and the truck they're renting, E'." Rafael says.

"Copy that. Why the helo? We know they're coming here."

"Lopez is scared of the Boss. He could tell Drew to drive back with Josh, and have the Pilot fly him somewhere with fifty gold bars."

"That's fifty million bucks." says Ethan.

"That would buy him a lot of protection."

There's a lot of activity behind the factory in Colver where workers are hastily loading gold bars into the helicopter under the Pilot's watchful 'weight count'.

"Pack 'em tight, guys. They can't shift during flight."

"Center of gravity, right?" says a worker. "My uncle's a pilot."

At the rear doors Lopez, Drew and Josh are hastily loading gold bars into the back of the rented eighteen footer when Lopez's phone rings. He takes it out and his face screams *Geez, not now*! He walks fifteen feet away for privacy.

"Lopez."

"One moment." snaps Helga, and seconds later -

"Your incompetence may cost me millions, Lopez!" shouts a distorted Kynsor.

"Sir, we're moving everything to Maple. The helo and the truck are loaded."

"Get my gold to Maple! I'll deal with your penalty later!" Kynsor snaps. The call is ended and Lopez looks at his phone. *Penalty*??

Everyone is so focused loading the gold they don't take note of a 'bird' flying overhead that dropped a PTC onto the truck roof, and is flying back to Ethan hiding behind a dumpster.

"Two PTC's on truck roof. Helo next."

"Copy that." says Raf. "How close are they to leaving?"

"Helo's still being loaded." tapping numbers on his HT keypad. "Doin' helo now." DB flies off and lands on top of the rotor shaft and deposits the PTC in the small, recessed area, and then flies off.

A worker is carrying a twenty-seven pounder to the truck. "Last one, sir." Lopez runs to the helo where Drew is with the Pilot.

"Boss called." looking at Drew. "He wants me to drive the truck to Maple."

Drew is surprised. "With Josh?"

"No, he wants both you guys at Maple A-SAP."

"What do you weigh, sir?" the Pilot asks him.

"One-eighty."

Pilot looks at Drew.

"What's Josh (weigh)?"

"Two-fifty."

"Two-fifty … plus you, minus one-eighty …" he enters numbers on his phone. "That puts us two hundred and seventy over safe load - you need to offload ten bars." Drew leans inside the helicopter and grabs a gold bar and hands it to Lopez, who turns and walks quickly towards the van. "Ten million more." he says under his breath, a small smile creasing his face.

Behind the dumpster, Ethan reacts to this activity.

"Guys, they're taking bars off the helo."

"Must be over their max." says Rafael. "How you doin', Mad?"
She's across the street from the factory, crouching behind bushes.

"Bored. I'm missing all the action." she grins.

"Oh, geez, they see me, guys!" Ethan's scared voice crackles via his DAC.

"Run, E'!" his sister gasps, not bored now!

Blue collar Sam is sweeping the floor in Franklin's front reception as Rafael rushes in from the smelting area, his hand over his mouth briefly. "Don't say a word, E!" he whispers, then looks sternly at Sam.

"I need you to call Drew right now!"
Sam senses it would be advisable not to ask why. He quickly has his phone out, hits a couple of numbers and hands it to Rafael.

"Hey, Drew, everything good?" seeing him on the video call.

"Yeah, all loaded up. Josh an' me are takin' the helo. Boss called Lopez, he wants him to … hang on, we caught a kid hangin' around." The video is jumpy for Rafael as Drew walks over to the dumpster where Ethan is firmly in Josh's grasp, beside Lopez.

"What are you doing here, kid?" Lopez demands.

"E, listen carefully to what I say and go with it." Rafael's voice crackles in Ethan's right ear.

"Hey, Drew, what's goin' on?" Drew's face is back on the screen.

"Lopez is grilling the kid what he's doin' here."

"Show me the kid." and now Ethan is on Raf's screen. "*Daniel?* What are you doing there?" Drew is quickly back on the screen. "You know him?"

"He's the Boss's kid."

"*What?!*" says Drew, stunned.

"Put the phone on him." Raf orders. Ethan's face again fills the screen.

"Daniel, did you overhear your father talking about the shipments?"

"Hey, dude." says Ethan.

"Say yes, E!" says Madison via her DAC.

"Yeah." looking sheepish.

"Okay, Daniel, I'm not going to tell your Dad. This never happened. No one saw you, okay?"

"Thanks, bro. When you comin' by the house? I miss hangin' with ya."

"I'll see you soon." gives him a thumbs up. "Put Lopez on." Lopez' face fills the screen.

"Thank God you called Drew." he whispers.

"He says you're driving the truck?"

"Yeah, go, figure, but he's the Boss, right?"

"I'll be waiting here for you, Lopez."

"Thanks, man." he puts his phone away and walks to Ethan, who's talking with Drew and Josh.

"Sorry for roughing you up a bit." Josh says, a nervous grin.

"It's okay, that's what my Dad pays you to do."

"Daniel, can we drop you anywhere?" asks Lopez.

"Naw, I'm cool. I'll catch an Ube'."

"You take care." Lopez smiles, leaning in for a gentle hug.

"Good luck, guys." Ethan says and he turns and walks away, grinning.

"Gonna join the Drama Club now, E'?" Madison's voices crackles in his ear.

"That was so much fun!" he whispers, walking across the lot.

"You did great." says Raf. "I got a feeling Lopez isn't coming here."

Lopez drives up in the truck and waves at Ethan as he passes. "He just drove past me in the truck."

"Was he alone?" Raf asks.

"Yeah, and he looked very happy."

"I think he's taking an early retirement with a golden bonus."

"As long as he's in the truck, I'll be tracking him." says Maya.

"Or his jacket's hangin' in his closet." grins E'.

"What? E', you're amazing!" chuckles Maya.

Lopez is on the phone as the truck passes the *Thank You For Visiting Colver* sign. He's very excited and speaking quicker than normal.

"Rent an eight by twelve foot unit … the kind where you can't see what's inside."

Rafael was right!

Maya's looking at the monitor to her left, where 'live' CCTV video plays showing Lopez's truck driving on a freeway.

"He's on the one sixty-five freeway, south."

"Copy. How's the video scrub goin'?" Rafael asks.

"Colver's done."

"Did you get the variety store E' was in?" Madison asks.

"That was the last one .. took longer to hack. I've wiped you walking up to Franklin's and inside reception, Raf'. Starting on the smelting area now." Looking at the monitor on her right showing video of Franklin workers placing single, gold bars inside several crucibles. The video stops when Rafael appears. Maya presses a tab and the video is fast-forwarded until Rafael is no longer on screen. The video stops. Maya taps on her keypad and the fifteen second video clip of Rafael is erased.

* * *

Seven hundred miles away in The Hamptons, Kynsor is in the den pacing, very worried.

"When has Lopez ever not answered your call?" he snaps at Helga, standing near him.

"There's been no reports on the News, sir."

"Don't think that, Helga! I'm hoping it's something else!" Then Helga's phone rings and Kynsor's face explodes with relief. Helga looks at the Caller I.D. and holds it for Kynsor to see. *Grigorski*.

Kynsor shakes his head vigorously. He doesn't want to talk to his gold buyer now!

***

The helicopter is cruising at two hundred and twenty-five kilometers an hour on its way to Maple Grove and Franklin's Furnace. Drew and Josh are looking at the gold bars, securely strapped in with leather belts.

"A buddy was flying supplies into Haiti a few years back." the Pilot says loudly over the roar of the rotors. "A strap broke an' his load shifted. Lost his CG an' that was it. Poor guy crashed." Drew shakes his head. "Never know when your number's gonna be called." Josh gives a gentle tug on the leather belt to confirm it's good. Drew takes out his phone and hits re-dial.

"Hey, Lopez, can you hear me okay?" he shouts.

"Yeah, how close are you?" Drew looks at the Pilot who flashes 5 fingers once.

"Five minutes. You making good time?"

"Should be there in about an hour an' a half"

"Okay." says Drew, ending the call. "I'm glad he's driving and not us, man." looking at Josh, then the Pilot. "He gets pulled over for speeding or a broken tail light, and the cop wants to check what's in the truck." he grimaces.

"Just two hundred million in stolen gold bullion, Officer." laughs Josh.

Maya is looking at Franklin's exterior security video playing on her monitor. A few keystrokes and the video vanishes.

"Okay, Franklin's scrubbed. You guys were never here, Raf."

He's standing with Madison and Ethan in the alley down the street from Franklin's. "Great, you can send your highlight package to the FBI."

"Copy that!"

"This is so exciting, guys!" says Madison, hugging Ethan and Rafael.

* * *

On the fourth floor of the FBI's Louisville Field Office two Agents rush up and enter the corner office of *Regional Director Howard Scott*. He's 45, short brown hair, in shirtsleeves, tie askew, seated at his desk. One of the Agents holds a sheet of paper, the other an opened laptop.

"Sir, we just received an encrypted e-mail with several video attachments clearly showing the gold bars."

"What?!" says the Director, quickly out of his chair and grabbing the e-mail. The Agent continues as Scott reads -

"It says this video was recorded at thirteen hundred hours today."

The second Agent places his opened laptop on the boardroom table and the Director leans close to the screen. It's the security video from Colver's property, showing Lopez, Drew, Josh and several workers hastily loading gold bars into the helicopter and the truck. The video jumps to the helicopter taking off … and cuts again to Lopez driving the truck and smiling at *someone to his left* as he drives past. The Agent pauses that video, and clicks another link to a new video showing Lopez and Drew running from the helicopter as debris kicks up.

"This is security video behind Franklin Furnaces in Maple Grove, which was recorded three hours before the Colver video."

"Absolutely incredible!" says the Director. "Any intel on who sent it?"

"No, sir, they knew how to cover their tracks."

"Get teams to Colver and Maple Grove … and not a word to the media!"

"Yes, sir." as he and the second Agent run out of the office.

* * *

Back in Maple Grove, Drew and Josh are in the smelting area of Franklin's Furnace where Sam's just told them they lost their power.

"Is it just in this area, Sam?" asks a stunned Drew.

"Think it's just us, sir." scratching his whiskers.

"You have a backup generator?!"

"Did … broke a few months back."

"Where's the nearest building supply store!?"

"Stevensville …'bout twenty miles north. The

young feller left fifteen minutes ago to buy one. Said to tell ya to wait here"

Drew is very relieved looking at Josh. "That dude's a smart guy." he smiles.

A quarter mile down the road from Franklin's a phalanx of FBI and State Trooper cruisers race past, sirens blaring and lights flashing, shocking several people exiting stores and vehicles. They pass three teenagers sitting on a bench, hoodies pulled up, sunglasses on, enjoying ice cream cones.

"It's going down, Maya!" grins Madison.

"Love to be a fly on the wall in there!" grins Ethan.

"Oh, yeah!" smiles Raf'.

Loud rock music is pumping in the smelter room so Drew and Josh haven't heard the sirens. Suddenly the door bursts open and a dozen F.B.I. agents and State Troopers rush in, guns drawn.

"FBI!! Put your hands on your head, and get down on your knees!"

Drew and Josh are stunned, and do as instructed as Agents rush to handcuff them.

* * *

Most of the residents of Maple Grove are across the street from Franklin's now because this small town hasn't seen this much excitement … *ever.* A dozen FBI and Kentucky State Troopers are out front, and two FBI helicopters are on the rear grounds. The entire property has 'Police Line Do Not Cross' Yellow tape around it keeping the hundred or so locals at bay, trying to grasp what's going on?

A hundred feet behind the throng, Rafael, Madison and Ethan are enjoying the fruits of what they orchestrated in less than forty-eight hours.

"Think they'll be able to arrest the Boss?" Madison asks.

"Hard to say." says Raf', licking his cone. "Lopez said he never met him, never saw his face, doesn't know his name and he distorted his voice on all their calls." He lowers his head as an F.B.I. vehicle drives past with Drew in the back, followed by a second vehicle transporting Josh.

"Wish we could be there when the FBI arrests Lopez." grins Ethan.

* * *

Eighty-five miles from Colver, Lopez is wearing a hoodie and sunglasses and keeping his head lowered as he walks past a security camera at a storage facility. He stops and reaches up with his left hand, while turning his head to the right, away from the camera as he sprays the lens with black paint. Then he runs to the truck and pulls up the sliding door. He climbs inside and grabs two gold bars. He's smiling from ear to ear as he runs to his newly rented storage unit, when there's a loud roar of sirens. Lopez is so shocked he drops one of the bars and it lands on his foot. *Owwww*!!! He screams in terrible pain, and drops the other bar to the ground. He sits on the floor and begins to cry, because he knows the excruciating pain in his foot is nothing like the pain he's about to experience as FBI Agents in windbreakers rush in, guns drawn.

* * *

An hour later two Agents are interviewing Josh at the FBI Field Office in Louisville.

"Drew told me the boxes contained stolen iPhones. I thought, okay, no big deal, their insurance will reimburse them, right? But when I learned it was the stolen gold bars, I said, 'hey, man, this is real serious, I can't be involved.' So Drew told me *they* would kill me if I didn't stay the course." The Agents look at each other. *Really?*

Down the hall two Agents are interviewing Drew in a small room.

"Lopez said he had a tip about a transport truck loaded with fresh produce. He asked if I wanted to make an easy five hundred for a night's work. I said sure. Well you can imagine my shock when we got back to the warehouse and I saw what was in the transport." The Agents look at each other. *Really?*

In another room two Agents are with Lopez.

"I never met the man .. never saw his face .. never heard his name, and when we spoke on the phone he had one of those voice distorters. I also spoke several times with a real snarky woman who covered her face with a Halloween mask …

***

Back in The Hamptons, Kynsor is in his den pacing nervously, changing Channels on every TV as he seeks News about gold bullion arrests. Suddenly his Channel-surfing lands on 'Breaking News' splashed over the screen. Kynsor stops pacing and listens to Lyla Wiggons, who has FBI Special Agent David Kimble in the Studio.

"I understand the FBI have made arrests in the gold bullion robbery." Wiggons says.

"Noooooo!" Kynsor screams, the TV remote falling to the floor.

"Yes, Lyla, early this afternoon our Louisville Field Office received an encrypted e-mail with dramatic video showing individuals carrying the gold bars inside a facility to be melted down."

"Who would be taking video?!!!" Kynsor says, as Kimble continues.

"There were several short video clips of security video inside two businesses in small towns in Kentucky that melt gold, silver and other precious metals. One of these businesses was in possession of what initial reports indicate is about seventy-five per cent of the stolen gold bars. From what we can tell the gold was at the point of being melted down, which would have made it untraceable. But inexplicably, the power supply to the business was cut off an hour before we got the anonymous e-mail."

"How fortunate." says Lyla.

"Yes. When our Agents and local Police swarmed the facility, two key players in the robbery were waiting for a backup generator to arrive."

"My producer tells me we have video of those two key players' arrest."

Lyla and Kimble are replaced on screen by the video of Drew and Josh, handcuffed, being led to cruisers by FBI Agents and Police Officers.

"Is one of them Lopez?!" Kynsor looks at Helga, who shakes her head.

"Then we received a second encrypted e-mail alerting us to a third man at a storage facility eighty-five miles away." says Kimble.

"We have Police body cam footage of that arrest." says Lyla.

Video plays showing FBI Agents leading Lopez handcuffed, crying and limping badly at the storage facility. Helga gasps loudly as Kynsor looks at her.

"Is he Lopez!?" glaring angrily. Helga nods her head and he looks at the TV.

"Mr. Lopez had his wife rent the storage unit just hours earlier." continues Kimble. "He was going to hide over one hundred million in gold bars he had in the truck."

"Lopez was stealing my gold bars, Helga!"

"Disgusting, sir!"

"Don't worry, it'll be okay. He can't identify me! He doesn't know my name! Never saw my face! I distorted my voice!" He smiles, then looks at the TV.

"Do you believe Lopez is the mastermind behind the robbery, Agent Kimble?"

"At this stage, yes, we believe he is, Lyla."

"See, Helga!" Kynsor claps his hands, smiling. Then he frowns, "I'll have to return Grigorski's twenty-five million deposit .. that sucks … "

* * *

Dr. G. and his wife are having dinner on a terrace, enjoying the spectacular view of Rome. She leans in close and whispers, grinning.

"Three hours ago we were looking at the Great Barrier Reef, and now we're in Rome. I'm so proud of you."

"Thanks, Laura. I love how the kids are really embracing it. They're exploring cities around the world in a way no child could ever imagine. I can't wait to see their growth over the next few years."

"I know, I just hope they don't get bored with it."

"Hey, guys!"

They're very surprised to see Madison and Ethan walking up, looking great in a change of clothes. They stand for warm hugs.

"What a nice surprise! I'm so happy you decided

to come." Mom says as they sit.

"You made it sound so great." says Ethan.

"And we wanted to hear about the Great Barrier Reef?" says Madison.

"It was amazing, but I want to hear where were you when I called? It was very noisy. "
In Kentucky watching the F.B.I. arrest the gold bullion robbers. It was amazing!

"Do you want to tell them, E'?" smiles Madison.

"Sure, but first, you guys likely haven't heard the big news." he grins.

"What?" asks dad.

"The FBI caught the guys who stole the gold bullion."

"Really? They had no leads yesterday."

"They split the gold into smaller loads and drove it to …..?" Ethan looks at Madison, who's trying not to grin.. "Where was it again?"

"Um, I think it was Illinois, or maybe Kentucky."

"It was Kentucky, and …" he stops as Madison stands. "I have to use the washroom." she walks away, and now she can grin.

"Actually, I need to go, too … it was a long flight." he grins, as he runs to catch up to his sister.

"Almost as cool as Raf', huh?" big grin.

"Why would you talk about the robbery?" still grinning.

"Because I could tell you didn't have a LWL ready, and now we have time to think of one. So what'd we do today?" putting his arm around her.

Back at the table the parents are smiling, watching.

"I can't get over how close they've become since we started porting." mom says.

"Traveling and meeting new people changes you. They're experiencing things they never could have imagined a year ago."

"It's so exciting thinking where they'll go next and who they'll meet." she grins.

* * *

20. LET'S CELEBRATE!

Two weeks later Madison, Ethan and Dr. G are having breakfast watching TV. Lyla Wiggons is at the News desk with a special guest in Studio.

"Joining me now is FBI Special Agent David Kimble. Good morning David, I understand you have very exciting news concerning the five million dollar reward the Bank offered for the recovery of their one billion dollars in gold bullion?"

"Yes, it is a good morning, Lyla, and very exciting. Late last night we received an encrypted e-mail from the anonymous sources who provided the crucial evidence that led to the recovery of the stolen gold bullion. They have requested that the Bank distribute the five million dollar reward as follows; one million dollars to Doctors Without Borders to continue their great work around the world. One million dollars to Habitat for Humanity to continue their great humanitarian work. One million dollars divided equally among twenty women's shelters at the Bank's discretion. One million, nine hundred thousand dollars to provide scholarships for at need students at the Bank's discretion, and the last one hundred thousand dollars is to be paid to a Mr. Clive Borges of New Orleans." He looks at Lyla.

"We were all just speechless when we read this.

"I'm speechless, David. How do you explain it?"

"I can't. We thought the anonymous tip was from an individual who knew of the criminal enterprise and had a reason to report what he knew. But people like that don't turn down a five million dollar reward."

"It's mind-boggling." Lyla says.
Madison is standing at the sink rinsing her glass, sniffling. Ethan is looking at his PB and banana slices toast, sniffling.

"That's incredible, isn't it?" Dad says.

"Yeah, really." says Ethan, spreading more PB on his toast.

"Yeah it is, have a good day, Dad." says Madison as she walks out.

"You, too, dear." Dad stands and fist-bumps Ethan. "See you tonight." and walks out of the kitchen. When Ethan hears the front door close he runs out of the kitchen and races up the stairs to Madison's bedroom. He knocks twice on her door and she opens it, smiling through happy tears.

"Do you believe it?!" she yells. "They're talking about us, E'!" hugging him so tight.

"It's surreal what we did." he says.

"I'll text Maya, you text Raf' … see if they can talk now!" she says.

A minute later Maya's smiling face is on Madison's burner phone screen, and Rafael's is on Ethan's, looking at each other and Madison and Ethan.

"He named the charities and the money for Clive." says Madison, very excited.

"That's so exciting!" says Rafael. "It's going to help so many people!"

"We must celebrate!" Maya says.

"Yes, I can't wait to meet you, Maya!"

"I can't wait to meet you, Raf'!"

"Okay, you guys pick a date and we'll be there!" Madison says.

Three Time Zones, Rafael's shift work, and Madison and Ethan's classes delayed the celebration for ten days until this sunny afternoon at Maya's home … when Ammi and Papa are away for the day!

"It's so great to finally meet you in person, Maya." Rafael grins, leaning in for a long, warm hug, as Madison and Ethan watch.

"It's great to finally meet you, Raf'. I feel like I've known you for years."

"Me, too!" as he makes room for Madison to come in for a hug.

"This is a very special day, Maya!" hugging her tightly.

"The first of many, Mad'. Hey, E', how was your flight?" she grins.

"Successful!" he chuckles, hugging her tightly, as Maya laughs. "We should get inside in case a neighbor tells ammi or papa they saw me with friends out here."

"We sure don't want that." says Ethan, as they quickly go inside.

Moments later Maya is seated at her desk showing Rafael how she tracks vehicles with PTC's on CCTV.

"This is incredible, Maya!" looking at the four squares on her monitor showing vehicles driving in four cities.

"It's how I saw Sarah's kidnapper's face when he was stopped for the red light. I'll show you more later, because I can't wait for you guys to see this." She taps some keys on her keyboard, and a new video appears on one of her monitors. It's a woman, late 40's, sitting at a desk in her office. "She's the director of a women's shelter in New York that received fifty thousand dollars."

"We bought 40 beds, a 60 inch TV, and toys for the children, we're just so grateful." The video ends. Maya taps more keys and a new video plays on the monitor, showing two women and two men, late teens, sitting together.

"It's given all of us a shot at the American dream." says one of the young men.

"Yeah, now we have hope." says one of the women beside him. "We're very grateful."

"Yeah, and we're going to study very hard." says the other man.

"Are we ever! And we want whoever donated the money to know we won't let them down." says the second woman. "And we're going to pay it forward."

That video stops. Maya taps a few keys and another video plays, this one filmed in Africa, showing a doctor in a white coat surrounded by a dozen, smiling young boys and girls, and several older people, many of them wearing glasses.

"It will allow us to buy more equipment and mobile vans to reach those who need help in remote areas. This gift is truly life-changing for these people and we appreciate it very much." He smiles at the twenty people, their cue to say - "Thank you!" as they all smile and wave.

The video ends and Maya cues up another. It's Clive with his wife, Betsy, standing beside their truck in front of their apartment with a TV Reporter.

"When Clive tol' me we were gettin' a hunnerd thousand dollars I knew it was true cuz' he was crying so hard he could hardly get the words out."

"Mr. Borges, do you have any idea who this anonymous donor is?

"No, I don't. Gettin' my truck back was a miracle. Then I got a full-time job. Praise Jesus. We felt so blessed. So to receive this money, I still can't believe it."

"The Lord works miracles every day, and we are so thankful." says Betsy, holding her right hand over her heart, as Clive hugs her. The video freezes, and Maya looks at her three friends, who are speechless.

"We did that, guys .. we made it happen." she

says softly, humbly. They look at each other, letting it all sink in.

Later, they're in the front room, chatting.

"Papa's family was poor .. he earned everything through hard work. He taught me how to be tough, not just with my judo, but tough mentally." He grins at Ethan. "I'm not always gonna be able to save your butt with a phone call, E., so before our next case I'm gonna give you some basics tips."

"That'd be great, Raf', thanks."

"The way you dealt with Drew and Josh was incredible." says Madison.

"I owe Carlos a lot of credit. He's given me very good advice." He grins. "But if Maya didn't have the video of Drew and Josh putting up the signs", he shakes his head, "me salvó el pellejo … it saved my bacon."

"We're a great team." Ethan says.

"We are." says Madison. "When I think of all the dots that had to connect for Ethan and I to meet you and Raf, it's definitely not a coincidence." They look at each other, nodding their heads.

"I had just come out of a cafe when the guy stole your bag."

"If you came out a minute later, we never meet you or know about Maria." says Madison.

"If your parents didn't convince you to enter the IT competition, Dad would never have met you." says Ethan.

"Yes, and if I don't hear you and Madison talking outside my bedroom …"

"All that made us realize we had to let you try, Maya." says Madison.

"Even though it meant betraying Dad." Ethan says, looking at his sister.

"Which was the worst feeling *ever*."

"Yeah … and it's still there."

"Every day …" says Madison.

"But then we think of the people we've helped." Ethan says. "If Dad knew something he invented to help our family spend more time together, had helped so many people, we know he'd be very happy."

"And it's only four cases, guys." says Rafael.

"I know in my heart we were brought together to help people." Maya says.

"E' and I believe that, too, Maya."

"I'm getting chills thinking of all the people we're going to help." Rafael says.

"I am, too!" says Maya."

"I can't imagine what our lives will be like a year from now." says Rafael.

"I know," says Madison, now sombre, "but one thing I do know, guys," she looks at each of them, "our lives will never be the same."
They each nod their head, and then they smile.

* * *

ABOUT THE AUTHOR

I'm a proud Canadian born in Ottawa, our
Nation's Capitol. I moved to Toronto when I was
three - Mom, Dad and older brother, Peter, came
with me. We were a middle-class family in a
nice home where I learned to always treat people
with respect. I was an average student, more
interested in hockey and baseball. I never
showed any real aptitude for writing until my
late 20's after two years of taking Eli Rill's
acting workshops. I had been in some TV shows
and films and decided to try to write a
screenplay. Eli thought it was really good and he
encouraged me to go to Los Angeles, where he
was moving with his wife and son to work with
Lee Strasberg at his famed Actor's Studio. A few
months later I was in the Cast of a Play Mr.
Strasberg was producing with hopes of taking it
to Broadway. Being in this environment sparked
an idea for a film. I wrote the script, showed it to

Eli and Larry Mann, a fine actor and fellow Canadian living in L.A. Larry introduced me to a producer who set up a meeting with Lew Weitzman, a respected literary agent with his own Agency after several years with the William Morris Agency. Lew signed me! I was thrilled! So were Eli and Larry. A year later I was hired to write the TV Movie "*King's Gambit*", followed by writing for '*Inspector Gadget*'. A few years later I had my own production company producing TV Movies. I share this because you never know when an opportunity will come along and change your life. I had no training in writing, and had I known then how difficult this business is, I likely would never have taken that first step. My friends thought I was crazy flying off to Los Angeles, but Eli saw *something* in me, and that was all I needed. If you have a dream, don't be afraid to take a chance to pursue it, and never be afraid of failing because that's how you learn to get better. And it really helps if you're fortunate to have a great mentor … or three!

I hope you enjoyed '*How They Came To Be*' It's the first novel I've written, and I enjoyed the process. It's so different than writing scripts for TV. I'd love to hear your thoughts on the story, and who your fave is - Madison, Ethan, Rafael, or Maya? Drop by their Blog - www.the4midables.com - and let me know. If you're an aspiring writer and have a question you'd like to ask, Post it and I'll be happy to reply. I've started writing Book Two in the Series. "*Who Are* They?" will be published in December, 2024.

Getting a Series on Television is very difficult. There's so many talented writers creating great stories, many hoping to get produced as a Series. If you liked (loved!) '*How They Came To Be*', I would appreciate it if you could;

* **Post a Review** where you purchased the book, saying why you liked it.

* **If you're on social** please consider posting a photo of the book cover with a   few comments to share with your Followers.

* **Upvote your fave Reviews** for my book on Amazon. You can '*Like*' Reviews you like, which helps others discover it.

* **Ask your local or school Library** to consider adding it to their collection.

Netflix, Amazon, Disney, and Apple invest millions to launch a new Series. If a lot of people love '*How They Came To Be*', and are excited to read *"Who Are They?"*, it will make their decision easier.

That's all for now. I have to get back to "*Who Are They?*"

Keep on top of all the news!

WWW.THE4MIDABLES.COM

#booktok
#books
#tiktok

Have a Question for me?

INFO@THE4MIDABLES.COM

Study hard … have fun … stay safe!

www.ingramcontent.com/pod-product-compliance
Lightning Source LLC
Chambersburg PA
CBHW051438050726
47593CB00005B/1834